Frank: I heard my brother call, but I was busy picking my way through the rubble. Alice's voice seemed to come from different directions, but I had a feeling she was down and to my right.

"Frank, don't do this! It's not safe!" Joe's voice got closer, but I heard someone grab him from behind.

"Don't you go down there too," I heard Detective Cole's voice instruct gravely. "It's not stable, and it's not safe for anybody. He's not listening to reason right now."

Frank! Help me!

She was definitely down there. Wasn't she?

Frank!

I closed my eyes. My vision was a little blurry, and I suddenly felt weak, like I could fall asleep right there in the rubble.

Frank!

I opened my eyes with a start. What was I doing? Alice needed me!

THE HARDY BOYS

Undercover Brothers®

#1 *Extreme Danger*

#2 *Running on Fumes*

#3 *Boardwalk Bust*

#4 *Thrill Ride*

#5 *Rocky Road*

#6 *Burned*

#7 *Operation: Survival*

#8 *Top Ten Ways to Die*

#9 *Martial Law*

#10 *Blown Away*

#11 *Hurricane Joe*

#12 *Trouble in Paradise*

#13 *The Mummy's Curse*

#14 *Hazed*

#15 *Death and Diamonds*

#16 *Bayport Buccaneers*

#17 *Murder at the Mall*

#18 *Pushed*

#19 *Foul Play*

#20 *Feeding Frenzy*

#21 *Comic Con Artist*

Super Mystery #1: *Wanted*

Super Mystery #2: *Kidnapped at the Casino*

#22 *Deprivation House*

#23 *House Arrest*

Haunted: Special Ghost Stories Edition

#24 *Murder House*

#25 *Double Trouble*

#26 *Double Down*

#27 *Double Deception*

Super Mystery #3: *Club Dread*

#28 *Galaxy X*

#29 *X-plosion!*

#30 *The X-Factor*

#31 *Killer Mission*

#32 *Private Killer*

#33 *Killer Connections*

#34 *The Children of the Lost*

Super Mystery #4: *Gold Medal Murder*

#35 *Lost Brother*

Available from Simon & Schuster

THE HARDY BOYS

Undercover Brothers™

BOYS

FRANKLIN W. DIXON

#36 Forever Lost

BOOK THREE IN THE LOST MYSTERY TRILOGY

Aladdin

New York   London   Toronto   Sydney

ALADDIN
An imprint of Simon & Schuster Children's Publishing Division
1230 Avenue of the Americas, New York, NY 10020
First Aladdin paperback edition January 2011
Copyright © 2011 by Simon & Schuster
All rights reserved, including the right of reproduction
in whole or in part in any form.
ALADDIN is a trademark of Simon & Schuster, Inc., and related logo is a registered trademark of Simon & Schuster, Inc.
THE HARDY BOYS MYSTERY STORIES is a trademark of Simon & Schuster, Inc.
HARDY BOYS UNDERCOVER BROTHERS and related logo are registered trademarks of Simon & Schuster, Inc.
For information about special discounts for bulk purchases, please contact Simon & Schuster Special Sales at 1-866-506-1949 or business@simonandschuster.com.
The Simon & Schuster Speakers Bureau can bring authors to your live event. For more information or to book an event contact the Simon & Schuster Speakers Bureau at 1-866-248-3049 or visit our website at www.simonspeakers.com.
Designed by Sammy Yuen Jr.
The text of this book was set in Aldine 401 BT.
Manufactured in the United States of America 1210 OFF
10 9 8 7 6 5 4 3 2 1
Library of Congress Control Number 2010915025
ISBN 978-1-4424-0264-5
ISBN 978-1-4424-0265-2 (eBook)

TABLE OF CONTENTS

1.	Aboveground	1
2.	A Quick Nap	9
3.	The Lion Sleeps Tonight	16
4.	Intervention	23
5.	Happyland	34
6.	Stanley	44
7.	On the Run	54
8.	Memories	65
9.	Back Under	81
10.	Map Quest	87
11.	Motives Unknown	100
12.	Bear Habitat	107
13.	Just Keep Him Talking	117
14.	Going In	127
15.	Science and Logic	136
16.	Imperfect	148

Aboveground

"**Whoa**," I murmured, staring into the hole before me as the dust cleared and I could slowly make out what remained of the hatch I'd recently escaped, now a huge pit filled with rubble.

"*Whoa* is right," my brother, Joe, agreed, stepping up beside me and giving me a totally out-of-character mother hen expression. "Are you sure you're okay, Frank?"

"Okay?" I repeated hollowly. What was okay, these days? My head was pounding from the explosion we'd just witnessed, and just an hour or so before that, I'd escaped from a creepy underground bunker where I'd been held prisoner along with a bunch of kidnapped children and given mysterious psychiatric drugs to keep me quiet. To say that Joe and I had fallen down the Wormhole of Weird on this particular case was understating it a bit.

About a week before, Joe and I had landed about fifty miles outside Misty Falls, Idaho, where, in the last twelve years, eight children had disappeared while camping at Misty Falls State Park. The local police had done extensive investigations into every one of these disappearances, but found nothing. Eventually, once the remains of one of the poor children was found in an abandoned bear cave, the disappearances were dismissed as natural accidents. Local residents especially were passionate about the idea that nature could be dangerous, and all these poor city-slicker campers had just fallen victim to some very nasty, hungry bears.

That was all well and good—until one of the missing kids mysteriously reappeared in town. Justin Greer had been only five when he'd disappeared, but now he was back, seventeen years old and slightly wild. He claimed to have no memory of his parents, though he did start having a few flashbacks after spending days with them. And he had no memories of where he had been for the last twelve years. Add this to his slightly animalistic eating habits, and his tendency to wander out of the hospital and skulk in the bushes, and Justin was a puzzle like no other. My brother Joe and I—agents in an elite force of crime-fighting teens called ATAC—had been called in to help the local investigator, Detective Richard Cole, get to the bottom of all this.

What we'd found, though, had just made the whole situation more baffling. For four nights, Joe and I camped near the sites of the disappearances, terrified by nightly invasions and starting to wonder if something more unearthly than a bear was responsible for these kids' fates. (Well, Joe was starting to wonder that. I'm really much more logical than he is.) One of our guides, a crusty old park ranger named Farley, turned up murdered in his own cabin just as Joe and I realized that he was Justin's paternal grandfather. And the next morning, total chaos broke out. An actual bear attacked our campsite, swiping at Joe and forcing Detective Cole to take him to the local ER. And while he was gone, it got even creepier. I fell asleep, only to wake up and find Detective Cole's partner unconscious outside the tent—right before something hit me over the head and knocked me out too.

How long had it been since then? I hadn't known until Joe filled me in that I'd been missing for two days. I'd spent that time in this creepy underground bunker. I was kept in a tiny cell, fed sandwiches through a slot in the door a couple of times. Eventually I made friends with a little girl, Alice, who I'd soon realized was one of the kids who'd disappeared—the media has dubbed them the Misty Falls Lost. And when Alice realized I was willing to help her find her brother, whom she misses terribly, she offered to help me break out of there.

Which I'd done. I'd successfully crawled out of a hatch leading into the woods, and Joe was right there, having followed a bunch of stone trail markers to the hatch.

Then it had exploded.

With Alice, and who knew how many other kids, still inside the underground bunker.

"Frank?" Joe asked, frowning as he laid a hand on my shoulder. I realized I'd never answered him, lost in my own thoughts.

"I'm—I—" I was struck by a wave of dizziness and closed my eyes. The drugs—something Alice had called the "forgetting potion"—that had been pumped into my system in the hatch were probably still affecting me. How much of what I was experiencing was real, and how much was chemical?

"Frank, maybe you should sit down."

But that's when I heard it. For some reason it seemed much louder than Joe's voice. . . .

Help me, please! Frank!

I blinked and searched for the source of the tiny female voice: the rubble that remained of the hatch.

"Oh my gosh," I whispered, drawing nearer to the lip of the crater the explosion had created.

"Frank!" I heard Joe shout behind me.

"Is he okay?" I heard running footsteps and Detective Cole's voice as he questioned my brother. But none of that mattered to me right now.

"Alice?" I called.

Frank! Please! Help!

There was no question: The voice was coming from inside the rubble. Alice was probably trapped down there! The rocks, dirt, and hunks of concrete and metal that now filled the crater where the hatch used to lead to an underground chamber were surely dangerous, but I couldn't let Alice stay trapped down there, alone! What if the rubble shifted and crushed her? What if no one but me ever heard her cries and tried to get her out?

"Alice, I'm coming!" I yelled, climbing over the edge and into the crater. "Stay where you are! Wait for me!"

Frank!

Alice's voice mingled with the shouts behind me.

"Frank!"

Frank!

"My God, what's he doing?"

". . . looked to me like he heard something."

"Doesn't seem normal, like he's on something . . ."

"Frank!" I heard my brother call, but I was busy picking my way through the rubble. Alice's voice seemed to come from different directions, but I had a feeling she was down and to my right. Gingerly, I moved a big rock and then pushed on a huge chunk of concrete in front of me. If I could move it, I might be able to squeeze down a small opening that led below the rubble. . . .

"Frank, don't do this! It's not safe!" Joe's voice got closer, but I heard someone grab him from behind.

"Don't you go down there too," I heard Detective Cole's voice instruct gravely. "It's not stable, and it's not safe for anybody. He's not listening to reason right now."

Frank! Please!

I pushed hard on the slab of concrete, letting out a yell of exertion—the thing was *heavy!* After what seemed like hours it budged a few inches, just enough for me to squeeze past it and into the little opening that led below.

Frank! Help me!

She was definitely down there. Wasn't she?

Frank!

I closed my eyes. My vision was a little blurry, and I suddenly felt weak, like I could fall asleep right there in the rubble.

Frank!

I opened my eyes with a start. What was I doing? Alice needed me!

Carefully I tried to shrink myself small enough to fit into the tiny tunnel through the rubble. Behind me, I could still hear Joe and the policemen yelling for me to stop, it wasn't safe. And I knew it wasn't safe—I wasn't *crazy.* Any fool could see the rubble wasn't stable. But an innocent ten-year-old girl who'd already suffered enough heartache needed my help. ATAC agents are trained to risk our own lives to help those in need.

Frank!

Breathing slowly, I managed to squeeze myself down far enough to duck into the tunnel. Joe's shouts got louder, but there was no way I was turning back now. Alice's voice seemed louder now, closer.

Come get me! Please!

I carefully scooted down the tunnel. It got darker the farther I went, the layers of rubble shutting out daylight. After I'd gone about ten feet, a new sound filled my ears. Rumbling, like the sounds you hear right before a killer thunderstorm. I sucked in my breath. Was it about to . . . ?

But then I heard it. *Crash, slam, crash . . .* It was the rubble around me! Just then the rock I was standing on shifted, seeming to drop down from under me. I let out a scream as the world around me collapsed. Then something huge and heavy hit my head and the whole world went black.

A Quick Nap

I was becoming really, really familiar with Misty Falls Hospital. I sighed, squirming in my not-terribly-comfortable padded vinyl chair as I looked at my brother again, willing him to stir. It was about eight o'clock in the morning, and I'd spent an overnight vigil in Frank's hospital room. I still had no idea what had prompted my normally sensible bro to climb into a hole filled with unstable pieces of concrete, rock, steel, and dislodged earth. But climb in he had, and the ensuing collapse had left him knocked unconscious and seriously beat up.

Fortunately, while Frank was covered with bumps, bruises, and scratches, and while it didn't look like he'd be taking Pilates classes any time soon, it did look like he would be all right. He had a broken arm and a shattered wrist from a huge piece of concrete landing on him, but he had no internal injuries, and the bump to his head somehow hadn't bumped him hard enough to cause serious damage. Still, Frank was going to be relaxing in this comfy hospital bed for a few more days, which meant that I, once again, was working the Misty Falls Lost case alone.

Which was fine.

I mean, once Frank woke up, at least he'd be able to tell me what he'd seen in that creepy underground bunker.

And at least ATAC gives us good insurance.

I yawned, stretching my arms above my head and trying to move my spine in a way that would get the nasty kinks out of it. Sleeping on a chair is no fun. Right then, I would have given just about anything even to be back in the rustic tent where Frank and I had spent the first week of our time in Misty Falls. Even with the potential ghost lurking outside, it was still a lot more comfortable than where I sat now.

I closed my eyes again, wondering if I could get another hour or so of sleep before Frank woke. I must have dozed a bit, because when I opened my eyes again a pretty, dark-haired candy striper was leaning over Frank's bed. I sat up and blinked. "Chloe!" Frank and I knew this candy striper from our days observing Justin in the hospital; Chloe even seemed to have (hard as it was for me to believe) a little crush on my not-so-smooth-with-the-ladies brother. She'd always struck me as a sweet girl, and very concerned about Justin's health.

Chloe jumped a little at the sound of my voice. "Oh—Joe," she stammered, glancing over at me. Was it just me, or did she not look thrilled to see me? Maybe she just wasn't a morning person. I certainly knew what that was like. "How long have you been here?"

"Hours," I replied, sitting up and stretching. "I've been trying to catch some z's before Frank wakes up. I guess you heard what happened to him?"

Chloe nodded. She kept glancing at me, but her eyes would wander right back to Frank. It was like he was a magnet, drawing her gaze. She drew a little closer to his bedside, holding something up in her hand. For the first time, I noticed she was carrying a little plastic bag of IV liquid—something purplish.

"Don't you usually work the afternoon shift?" I

11

asked, recalling all our past encounters over Justin. "I'm surprised you're here this early."

Chloe nodded quickly at me, then turned back to Frank. "I, um . . . I switched my shift today." She flashed me a brief, toothy smile. "I have a family thing this afternoon. I just need to change Frank's IV. . . ."

As she drew closer to the pole where Frank's current IV bag hung, I noticed something: The purplish liquid she was planning to switch in didn't match the clear liquid he was hooked up to now.

"New color, huh?" I asked.

Chloe stopped short and looked back at me, a little startled. "What?"

"The IV bag?" I asked, standing up from the chair and stretching some more. "The old stuff is clear, but this is purple. Are you changing his medicine?"

Chloe glanced from me to Frank, then nodded again, quickly, and moved toward the pole. "It's a sedative," she replied, quickly changing out the bags. "Frank needs his sleep."

I frowned. Even in my groggy state, that didn't sound right. "He needs his sleep?" I asked. My brother had just been bonked on the head by a huge rock. And yeah, he was in for a world of pain when he finally woke up. But I needed him to wake up. I needed to ask him a few choice questions. Questions like, *What the heck happened down there, Frank? What did you learn about the Misty Falls Lost? How can you help me solve this case so we can go home?*

Chloe just glared back at me blankly. "Of course," she replied. The new IV bag was in place now, and she turned, looking satisfied at the sight of the purple liquid dripping into a vein on my brother's hand.

"According to who?" I asked after a moment. Were candy stripers even allowed to change IVs? I'd never seen her do this before.

Chloe looked at me like I'd lost my mind. "According to his *doctor*," she replied, shaking her head. "If you'll excuse me . . ."

And just like that, she took one last glance at my brother and darted out of the room.

Great, I thought, checking my watch with a sigh. It was just after eight thirty. And judging from the size of that IV bag, my brother would be out for hours now.

I blinked, glancing around my brother's cold, sterile hospital room. The sun was brightly peeking through the blinds, signaling the arrival of another new day. *Another new day and no closer to any answers*, I thought ruefully. At least I had my brother back now—beaten up, but safe and sound in the hospital. And once he woke up, I knew he would give me the scoop about everything he'd learned belowground.

And maybe we'd be a little bit closer to finding Justin again and solving this case.

I sighed, shaking my head. It was no use sitting back down in that miserable chair; I was wide awake now. I decided to walk down to the nurses' station and see whether they could find Dr. Klaus, the doctor who'd treated Frank in the emergency room. I could ask him about this sedative business and find out how long he planned to keep my brother unconscious. And then maybe I could run back to the B and B where I was staying and grab another couple hours' sleep before coming back to the hospital.

Just as I exited Frank's room, though, my phone beeped. I pulled it out, wondering if it was some kind of urgent message from ATAC headquarters. But instead, the name that flashed on my incoming text message was DETECTIVE RICHARD COLE.

WE NEED TO TALK. MEET ME AT MY OFFICE.

Detective Cole wasn't one for exaggerations—so this sounded urgent.

Dropping my phone back into my pocket, I headed to the exit, wondering what could possibly happen next.

The Lion Sleeps Tonight

"Isn't this nice?" Chloe asked me as we snuggled together on a crude wooden raft, the water from the river sloshing gently against the sides. I sighed and closed my eyes. It *was* nice—a little weird, but nice. Above us, a crystal blue sky was dotted by the occasional white, puffy cloud. And cute little cartoon birds flitted around, singing . . . singing . . .

"The Lion Sleeps Tonight"?

"Whee dee dee dee oh whee dee dee dee we um weem a way . . ."

The raft rocked gently as we floated down-river. I don't know how much time passed—it felt like time had slowed down somehow, like we'd always been floating on this raft together. Chloe squeezed my hand and I opened my eyes to smile at her.

"I'm so glad you're okay," she said, looking at me with concern in her eyes. "I was worried about you. I want—"

Just then, a loud *sploosh* drew my attention to the water, and I sat up, my mouth dropping open in surprise. There, in the water, clinging to the side of the raft hand and holding out two tuna sandwiches in plastic bags, was a soaking-wet Alice. She still wore a pale pink nightgown and her princess tiara, and she looked a little disappointed in me.

"Are you awake yet?" she demanded of me, her blue eyes huge in her small, worried face. "Are you going to help me or not?"

My eyes flipped open to reveal a dingy white ceiling. I heard machines bleeping and blooping, and smelled the stark, antiseptic smell of institutional cleaner. I blinked a couple times, then glanced sideways, where I spotted a very surprised—almost frightened-looking—Chloe, perched in an uncomfortable-looking plastic seat. In her hands she clutched a beat-up copy of *The Adventures of Tom Sawyer*, open to the middle. On a small white

Formica table, a portable radio pumped out staticky oldies.

"*Whee dee dee dee dee dee dee dee dee dee . . .*"

I took a deep breath.

I was in a hospital.

Why?

But as soon as my brain asked the question, my body answered it. *Pain.* It was vague and dulled, but my arms still felt sore, like they'd been buried under a pile of bricks. And my head pounded. Above all, though, I felt so, *so* sleepy. I blinked again and shook my head, trying to force myself awake.

I turned to Chloe, who was still watching me curiously, like I was an animal in the zoo. She looked nervous.

"Where am I?" I asked, reaching up to rub my eyes. My left hand had a needle sticking into it, feeding in purple liquid from a hanging IV. The bag was almost empty. "What happened?"

Chloe sprung to her feet, looking unsure of what to do. For some reason, my question seemed to make her even more uncomfortable. "Um," she said, her eyes darting around the equipment that surrounded me, looking everywhere but into my eyes. "Hey, Frank . . . how do you . . . feel?"

She picked up a small white plastic object from

the table next to me and began rapidly pressing a button. Was she calling a doctor? I shook my head again, fuzziness spreading into the edges of my vision. Where *was* I?

"I feel like . . . like I've been hit by a truck," I replied slowly, the words feeling strange and unwieldy in my mouth. I looked around the room: definitely a hospital room. But what had happened to me? Why did my arms hurt? Why was—I noticed now—why was my left arm and wrist in a cast? "Where's Joe?" I asked finally, desperately wishing my brother were here to explain things.

"Oh, Joe's . . . around," Chloe replied, rapidly hitting the button a few more times. "You know. He had some sort of errand to do. In town."

That sounded weird. Joe didn't do "errands," and it wasn't like him to leave his unconscious brother alone in a hospital bed. Maybe he was working on something for a . . . case? Were we working on a case?

"You're awake." A sharp, deep voice invaded my thoughts. I looked up in time to see a dark-haired man in a white lab coat enter the room and stride purposefully toward the bed. Strange: He appeared to be a doctor—*my* doctor?—and yet he didn't seem happy about my being conscious at all.

I squinted at him. "Who are you?" The guy

looked strangely familiar, but I couldn't place him. He didn't answer me, though, just checked my IV (still connected, still dripping) and frowned more deeply.

"I thought I told you to give him the full bag of purple fluid," the doctor said, glaring at Chloe. "That should have kept him asleep for at *least* two more hours."

"I did!" Chloe insisted, jumping to the doctor's side like she was afraid of him. "And I've been playing music, reading to him, trying to be soothing, but he woke up anyway."

I leaned back against my pillow, my mind wandering. Whatever was in that purple IV, it was definitely making it hard for me to focus. Mysterious IVs . . . sedatives . . . Alice . . . Suddenly images started flooding my brain, and I sat straight up as it all started piecing together.

Alice. The facility underground. I was kidnapped from our campsite and . . .

"You were there!" I cried suddenly, using all my strength to point an accusing finger at Chloe. "In the underground bunker with me! You saw what was happening to all those kids, being drugged and sedated! Where's Alice?"

Chloe looked stricken. I could tell from her immediate reaction that she knew exactly what

I was talking about. She paled, and her mouth fell open as she looked to the doctor for assistance. All at once I remembered his name too. *Dr. Carrini.* He'd been treating Justin, the kidnapped boy who'd mysteriously reappeared in town with no memory of the last twelve years. Justin was the reason ATAC had sent Joe and me to Misty Falls, Idaho. We were supposed to be getting to the bottom of what happened to him. But so far, every discovery we'd made had just led to another cluster of unanswerable questions.

I was so busy watching Chloe that I was startled by two hands clasping the sides of my face and pulling me close to Dr. Carrini.

"You're talking nonsense," he told me, his voice low and gravelly. "That's why I asked to replace Dr. Klaus as your doctor. When you were being treated in the trauma room, you were babbling incoherently about what you'd supposedly seen. You've clearly been given some drugs that are producing false memories. An underground bunker where kids are kept hostage? Mysterious medical treatments and drugs? That would make an excellent science fiction movie. But it's not real," he scoffed.

Memories. That's why Dr. Carrini had been treating Justin: He was some sort of nationally recognized expert on memory and recovering repressed memories. Since Justin claimed to remember nothing, Dr. Carrini had been called in to help. But he was especially concerned about "false" memories, which he'd cautioned that Justin might be reporting in an effort to please his parents.

I tried to sit up. "It *was* real!" I insisted, looking desperately at Chloe. I knew that for sure: *My* memories were not false. *You were there!* "I remember! I—"

But before I could finish, Dr. Carrini pulled a hypodermic needle out of his chest pocket and violently jabbed it into my arm. I stiffened, stunned, wanting to fight him off, but I was too weak from whatever was in the purple liquid to move quickly, and within seconds, a warm, deadening sensation ran through my veins, making it impossible to do anything but go limp against the pillows.

"That's it," I heard Dr. Carrini say as the fight went out of me. "Just calm down. This will put you out for a good, long time."

But I don't want that! I want to be awake, I want to find Joe, I want to find out what happened to . . .

Before I could even complete the thought, though, the room went dark, and soon Chloe and I were drifting off on the raft again.

ntervention

I called a cab to take me to the Misty Falls police station, which was in downtown (if a stoplight and a couple of stores qualified as a downtown) Misty Falls and a few miles away from the hospital. When I walked in, the young man working the reception desk gave me an odd look—part suspicious and part sympathetic.

"Detective Cole's waiting for you down the hall in the conference room," he said, gesturing to the hallway on his right.

Conference room? It seemed a little odd that Detective Cole would require such a large room to meet with just me, so I wondered if there might be a couple of other people involved. When I turned the corner to enter the conference room, sure enough, my breath caught. On one side of the table sat a tired and frustrated-looking Detective Cole; on the other side, sitting all in a row like a firing squad, were Jacob Greer, Justin's father; Donna, his young, pretty girlfriend; and Michael Smith, the arrogant private investigator they'd recently hired to find the missing Justin.

"Well hello, Joe," Detective Cole greeted me with weariness in his voice.

I stepped into the room, nodding, as Jacob, Donna, and Smith all turned to glance at me. Jacob openly scowled. Donna just watched me blankly. And Smith smirked, shook his head, and looked back at the table. Last I saw him was the night before, when I'd sort of maybe been kind of stealing his motorcycle, which I later crashed, so I guessed I could understand his not rolling out a welcome mat. The apparent scorn of Jacob and Donna, though, was a little more surprising.

"What's up?" I asked.

Detective Cole cleared his throat. "Have a seat," he said, gesturing to the chair next to his.

I sat, getting an eyeful of what Detective Cole must have been facing for the last few minutes: three very challenging, unimpressed faces.

"It seems," Detective Cole began, "that Jacob,

Donna, and Smith have some concerns about how I've been handling their case."

Jacob snorted, pulling his flannel shirt tighter around him. He was tall and bearded, with salt and pepper hair, and at the moment, he looked like an angry lumberjack. "That's an understatement."

I frowned. "Why are you upset?" I asked, honestly not getting it. "We had a major breakthrough in the case last night. We found my brother, coming out of some sort of hatch in the woods. He told us about the system of underground tunnels where he'd been taken from our campsite—and he saw some of the Misty Falls Lost there!"

Jacob glared at me, and Michael Smith openly scoffed. "An underground system of tunnels, eh?" he asked, smirking at me like the very idea was ridiculous. "Some kind of underground laboratory where eight children could be kept undetected for over a decade? And so that whoever's keeping them could—do what with them?"

"I don't know," I replied honestly. "That's why we have to find where this hatch led to, and ask my brother for more information when he wakes up." I glanced at Detective Cole, explaining, "They've got him sedated right now, under orders from his doctor. Maybe later you and I could go over there and—"

"Ex*cuse* me," Jacob broke in, slamming his hand down on the table. "I think I came in here to talk about my missing son. Can we please focus on my missing son?"

I turned to look at the gruff, angry man. Since we'd met him a week ago, Jacob had struck Frank and me as a little rough around the edges—awkward, easily angered, even a little mean. I still wasn't sure whether this was because Justin's reappearance was stressing him out so much, or because he had something less savory to hide. According to Justin's mother, Jacob had never been an ideal father, and their relationship had dissolved soon after Justin went missing. As far as I could tell, though, Jacob truly loved his son—he just had an incredibly awkward way of expressing it.

Detective Cole reached out his hand toward Jacob. "Listen, Jacob," he said soothingly, "nobody's forgotten about Justin. Getting him back safely to you is my number one priority. But I truly believe that what we saw in the woods last night could be the key to—"

Smith cut him off with a snort. "And what exactly *did* you see in the woods last night?" He looked challengingly at Detective Cole, then me, almost daring us to answer.

"Well . . . ," I began, but Detective Cole held up a hand to stop me.

"As I've already told you," the detective told Jacob in the same calm, controlled voice, "Joe saw his brother emerge from a trapdoor in the ground, and approximately one hour later, when my officers and I arrived on the scene, there was an explosion. The trapdoor and the tunnel Frank described below were destroyed. But from what Frank told us—"

"So there's no evidence," Smith cut in again, glaring at Detective Cole.

Detective Cole waited a beat before responding. "There is . . . there is a hole dug out by the explosion," he insisted.

Donna snorted now, twisting her mouth into an angry smirk. "But what connects that hole to Justin?" she asked, looking from Detective Cole to me. "Just the ravings of some druggie kid. No offense." She shrugged in my direction.

It took me a minute to figure out her meaning. *Druggie?* Wait a minute. . . .

I laughed out loud. I couldn't help it. "Ma'am . . . no offense to *you*, but my brother is about the furthest thing from a druggie you could imagine. He won't even take medicine for a cold because it makes him drowsy."

Smith folded his arms, turning to face me. "I suppose that's why the hospital says he had five different drugs in his system when he was admitted."

I glanced at Detective Cole. Was that true? The detective nodded slightly, with a little shrug. *Well, that's not Frank's fault,* I thought.

"He was being held captive," I said, responding to Jacob now. "He says the people down there gave drugs to the kids to keep them quiet and manageable."

"Either way, why should we trust him?" Donna asked. "He was still high as a kite. Who knows if what he remembers was real?"

I took a deep breath. "Really," I said, "my brother is one of the most trustworthy—"

But Jacob cut me off, holding up his hand. "All right," he said. "Let's look at what your brother is saying. What is that?"

I swallowed, thinking back. "He . . ." Well, the truth was, Frank himself wasn't terribly sure what he'd seen in the underground bunker. When I'd first asked him where he was coming from, his response had been *I have no idea.* "He said it was an underground bunker of some kind. He was kept alone in a small room for a long time, being fed sandwiches through a slot in the door, with no outside contact. Finally he befriended a little girl, Alice, who he believed to be one of the Misty Falls Lost. And eventually, when he got out of the room, he saw that other Misty Falls Lost were living there too—including Justin." I paused. "He said there were different medical personnel there too, including a big guy they called Baby Doc. . . ."

I trailed off. Jacob was rolling his eyes now, Smith was staring down at the table, shaking his head, and Donna snorted again. I sighed, wishing it all made more sense. But I knew it was true. I trusted Frank. Even under the influence of whatever drugs they'd had him on, he wouldn't make something like this up.

"Is there a problem, Jacob?" Detective Cole asked. I could hear the frustration in his voice, and I felt it too. Here we were, so close to finally finding out what happened to Justin, and Jacob was questioning it. Why?

Jacob shifted in his seat, stamping his foot onto the floor with a *bang!* that made us all jump. "You're darn straight, there's a problem," he replied, looking from Detective Cole to me. "Underground bunkers? Kids being held for years, for no reason? Mysterious doctors, doing . . . who knows what? Handing out cocktails of drugs to children?" He shook his head. "This isn't an episode of *Lost*, men, this is my son's life. His *life*."

He paused for a minute, and Detective Cole began, "We understand that, Jacob—"

Jacob slammed his hand down on the table, cutting the detective off. "No you don't! *No you don't*," he insisted, glaring at Detective Cole. "Do you have kids, Detective?"

The detective looked surprised. "No," he said after a moment. "No, but—"

"Then you can't possibly know how I feel," Jacob continued. "I've lost my son. *My son.* Not once, but thanks to you and your sorry excuse for a police force, twice."

Detective Cole winced.

"And now," Jacob went on, pointing at the detective, "you're trying to sell me some two-bit science fiction movie to explain where my son went from that hospital. Well, *I'm not buying.*" He stood up, glancing at Donna, who quickly followed suit. Smith stood up too, smirking vaguely, and all three glared down at us.

Jacob frowned at the detective for a few more seconds, then nodded at me and silently stalked out. Smith shook his head in my direction—I gulped, remembering his wrecked bike from the night before—and then all three walked out of the station.

There was silence for a minute as the detective and I thought our private thoughts.

"I saw it," Detective Cole said finally. When I looked up questioningly, he went on, "I saw that hatch, son. I believe your brother is telling the truth."

I nodded. "So do I," I agreed. "But for some reason, Jacob doesn't even want us to look into it."

Cole stood up. "Well, we most certainly *are* looking into it," he insisted. "I've got a team of officers out there right now, looking for clues in the rubble. But we need more information. We need to talk to Frank."

I nodded, sighing. "But they've got him sedated," I said with a frown. "His doctor thinks he needs his rest or something. We're so close to cracking this case wide open, and the only person who could give us some clues can't talk to us."

Detective Cole nodded, looking thoughtful. Then his expression suddenly brightened, and his eyes seemed to dance in his head. "Well," he said, standing up, "not the *only* person."

I stared at him. "What do you mean?"

He smiled. "Follow me, son."

I stood, and he led me out of the little conference room and down the hall. I realized that we were heading into the jail section of the police station, the few cells where criminals were held before being transferred to a state facility. We walked by a cell filled with biker types who glared at us as we passed. In the next cell, a small body sat huddled on a cement bench. When we paused in front of the bars, a messy head of black hair raised itself, and we were suddenly looking into a pair of dark, piercing—and slightly familiar—eyes.

"That's Stanley, the kid who ran into the hospital with the knife a couple of days ago," I realized, looking at him. He was a little older than Frank and me, college-age maybe, with a wild, slightly unhinged look. He'd run into the hospital cafeteria with a butcher knife, demanding to see Justin. Of course, that was when Justin was still *in* the hospital, before he'd disappeared—maybe to the same underground bunker where my brother had been held. Stanley had refused to tell us anything about who he was or why he needed to see Justin, so Cole had arrested him.

"Correction," said Detective Cole, looking at the kid with satisfaction. "Let me introduce you to Stanley Stapleton."

I blinked. "Stapleton?" I asked. "Why does that sound familiar?"

Detective Cole turned to me and smiled. "From all your research into the Misty Falls Lost, I reckon," he replied. "Remember one of the most recent victims—Alice?"

I gasped. Of course! Alice—the girl my brother had been babbling about seeing in the bunker when he'd crawled back into the rubble and gotten himself beaned in the head.

Detective Cole nodded, seeing the recognition in my eyes. "This is Stanley," he told me, "her brother."

Happyland

"**P**ass the cotton candy, please." I smiled and looked up from a plate piled high with ice cream, chocolate kisses, and cupcakes. Alice was sitting next to me at a huge dining room table, smiling in her princess outfit and revealing two missing front teeth. At the end of the table, three different televisions were tuned to three different cartoons, and the other kids around the table paused every so often in their loud chewing to watch.

"The pink or the blue?" I asked, gesturing to two different serving dishes, each filled to the brim with fluffy sugar.

Alice snickered. "The pink, of course," she replied. "It matches my outfit."

That made perfect sense. I passed her the cotton candy, then reached into a bowl of circus peanuts and took a big handful for myself. "It's strange," I said, "but I feel like we've been eating candy for hours, and I don't feel at all sick to my stomach."

A teenage boy next to me snorted. I turned to look at him and realized that it was Justin, licking a huge, swirly lollipop. "Nobody gets sick in Happyland," he explained. "Here, we're kids forever, and we don't have to worry about stupid adult things like nutrition."

"That's right," a female voice chimed in from across the table. I turned toward its source and jumped—a small, child-size skeleton was sitting there, popping Cracker Jacks into its mouth! "Here in Happyland, we get to have an eternal childhood!"

A boy of about ten years old who sat next to the skeleton shook his head. "Well, except for you, Sarah," he said, looking at the skeleton with affection. "Ever since that bear got you, you've been looking a little . . . bony!"

The skeleton groaned and threw popcorn at the boy. "You keep your jokes to yourself!" she chided. "It's not my fault—"

But before she could continue, something changed in the room. A shadow seemed to fall over it, like a cloud had passed over the sun. The joyful mood around the table drained abruptly, and soon I realized that everyone was staring at a door to the left, where two full-grown men stood. Two strangely familiar full-grown men . . .

"Baby Doc," Alice whispered, fear thickening her voice. "It's time for our hurty medicine."

Just then, Baby Doc pulled a syringe from behind his back and held it up, pushing the plunger so a purplish drop of liquid medicine squirted from the top. "Who's first for forgetting?" he asked, looking around the table. Behind him, the other guard—who I heard the other kids call "Scar"—pulled five or six syringes from his lab coat pocket, cackling cruelly.

"Step right up, kids!" he called, fanning the syringes out in his hand. "Good little children don't remember their families. . . ."

None of the kids moved. It seemed to me we were all feeling too scared. But Baby Doc and Scar didn't let that stop them as they charged into the room, grabbing the kids out of their seats and jabbing needles into their arms.

"Take your medicine!" Scar screamed, as he grabbed the young boy who'd been sitting next to the skeleton and shot him up with the purplish medicine. The boy howled in pain, but the sound had barely escaped his lips when he crumpled to the floor at Scar's feet, fast asleep.

One by one, Scar and Baby Doc made their way around the table, shooting each kid in the arm and putting them to sleep. Even Sarah the skeleton somehow got a shot and promptly fell to the floor. I backed away, panicked, searching the room for any place to hide, but there was nowhere. Baby Doc grabbed Alice as she shrieked. Then suddenly Scar appeared before me, grabbing my arm and holding the syringe high.

"Say good night," he hissed through gritted teeth.

"*Nooooo!*" I screamed. . . .

Beep. Beep. Beep. Beep. I blinked against the bright sunlight, suddenly coming to in the same hospital bed I'd been in before. Was it all a dream? From the angle of the sun streaming through the window, it looked to be early afternoon.

I rubbed my eyes and glanced around, my eyes pausing on the IV still hooked to my right arm. A tiny amount of purple liquid remained in the bag, slowly dripping into my IV. Barely giving myself enough time to think it through, I grabbed the needle in my injured hand and yanked it from my right arm. A sharp, stinging pain immediately spread from the inside of my elbow outward, and I pushed a wad of bedsheet against the wound to stop the bleeding. *Yeowch!* It hurt a lot, but the pain was better than whatever "forgetting" medicine Dr. Carrini had been pumping into me. I'd spent too much time wasting away in this hospital bed. It was time for me to find my brother and get back on the case.

I glanced around the room, pleased to find it empty except for me. The radio that Chloe must have brought in still sat on the bedside table, playing staticky oldies, and a magazine—*Popular Science*—was open on a plastic chair, where I imagined Chloe had been reading it to me. But she was gone now—maybe taking a break, or maybe she'd been called to some other candy-striper duty. Either way, it meant the same thing.

This was my chance. I had to get out of this hospital without anybody noticing.

Slowly I sat up. The room spun, and my arm ached in the bulky cast, but I stopped and blinked and tried to pull it together. I was still weak, clearly, from either the accident or the drugs I'd been given—who knew which? But all I had to do was make it out of the hospital. After that, I could find Joe and Detective Cole and get medical care somewhere else—from someone else. It was clear to me that Dr. Carrini wasn't going to help me. He was too obsessed with my so-called "false memories"—just like he'd accused Justin of having. Except my memories were anything but false. Which implied to me that Justin had been telling the truth about his parents and what he remembered from the night he'd disappeared as well.

Carefully I swung my legs over the side of the bed and put my feet on the floor. The room spun again, but I quickly regained my bearings. Working as hastily as I could with one bum arm, I ripped a small strip of sheet from the bed and tied it around my arm where the wound from the IV remained. It was still bleeding, but it seemed to have slowed. Hopefully it wouldn't draw attention to me.

I looked around for my clothes but couldn't find them. It looked like I'd be making my escape in this oh-so-fashionable hospital gown. Oh, well. I stood slowly, waiting for the room to realign, and then tiptoed over to the door. Careful to avoid being seen, I peered out into the hallway, and when I saw no one, I leaned my head out and looked up and down the hall. The coast was clear. This was my shot.

I darted into the hall, moving as quietly as I could, and slipped through the door to an emergency stairwell. Pausing to catch my breath, I tried to remember the layout of the hospital from when Joe and I had come to see Justin. On the ground floor was a huge cafeteria; beyond that, the emergency room and exit to the parking lot. I didn't have far to go. I took a deep breath and ran down the stairs, peering out onto the ground floor.

The cafeteria was busy—filled with doctors, visitors, nurses, and volunteers. It had to be right around lunchtime. Even a few patients like myself, dressed in hospital gowns or pajamas, milled around with their families. *Good,* I thought. *I won't attract too much attention.*

The hallway led straight by the cafeteria, down past the admitting desk of the emergency room, and out the door. It was bright and wide. If I could move fast enough, I could easily get out without anyone blocking me. I took another deep breath. *This is it,* I told myself. *Time to get out of here, find Joe, and find out what's really going on.*

Swinging the door open, I ran. My legs pumped like pistons, rocketing me forward as fast as I could possibly go.

"Hey!" I heard behind me, a few surprised voices in the cafeteria probably wondering why this crazy, half-naked person in a cast was zooming by. "What the—?"

"Is he okay?"

I kept running, keeping my focus on the exit. I was almost past the cafeteria now. Just a few more yards . . .

"Frank?" Footsteps ran up beside me, and suddenly a hand clamped down on my right arm, digging into the area where the IV had been with tiny, sharp fingernails. "*Frank?*"

The sharp pain of fingernails near my wound nearly threw me off balance, but it held firm. I stumbled to a stop and turned. "Chloe?" *Oh, man. I was so close. How do I get out of here now?*

"Where are you going? Are you okay? Let me page Dr. Carrini." She moved toward the wall, to a nearby phone, but now I grabbed *her* arm to stop her. Part of me wondered if I should just push her aside and book it to the door. But—no. She wasn't Dr. Carrini, and she didn't have the strength to hold me here by herself. And I still needed answers from her. I still needed to know what had really happened to me.

"Chloe," I said, looking her in the eye. "Listen to me. I need you to be honest with me. What happened to us in that bunker? What's going on down there? What happened to all those kids?"

Chloe looked down, refusing to meet my eye. "Frank, you're—you're talking nonsense."

"I'm not," I insisted. "You were there with me, Chloe. You said I would be a 'permanent resident.' If I had stayed, I would have been your 'special responsibility.' What does that mean?"

Chloe still wouldn't look at me. "These—these must be the false memories Dr. Carrini was talking about," she said in a small voice.

"Stop lying," I hissed, getting impatient now. *Why wouldn't she tell me the truth?* "What are you hiding, Chloe? Who are you working for? What happened to all those kids—the Misty Falls Lost? You *know*, don't you?"

Chloe met my eyes finally, looking conflicted. She was obviously struggling with whether to answer my questions. Finally she opened her mouth—and my heart quickened. Would she tell me the truth? Could I possibly win her over to my side? Would she help me find those kids again?

But then, suddenly, Chloe let out an ear-splitting scream. "HELP! HELP ME! This patient is threatening me, trying to escape! HELP!"

I was stunned. *She's betraying me!* But still, I waited only a second before springing into action. I had to get out of there. Security guards ran up to me from both sides, but I managed to dart around one and ran as fast as my legs would carry me to the exit. All my dizziness subsided as pure adrenaline took over. I heard shouts all around me, and I had to dodge a few confused-looking nurses, but I made it to the doors and pushed them open, tumbling into the bright sunlight.

The security guards were still trailing me, but I had a good lead now. I booked it across the hospital lawn toward the woods, not letting myself think about anything except getting one foot in front of the other and *moving, moving, moving.* After what Chloe had done, there could be no mistake.

My only chance of getting to the bottom of this case—and maybe ever getting my freedom again—was to escape this hospital.

Stanley

"**S**o you're Alice's brother?" I asked, sitting down across from Stanley in the cell. He recoiled, looking almost stricken at his sister's name. I glanced at Detective Cole, who gently put a hand on Stanley's shoulder.

"It's okay, Stanley," he told the boy. "Joe is a friend. You can trust him."

Stanley turned to me, his eyes piercing in their intensity. "You know where Alice is?" he asked.

"Not yet," answered Detective Cole, "but we've been trying to find her. That's who you've been asking for?"

Stanley looked at him, then quickly down at the

floor, hugging himself. "I have to find her, I have to find her, I have to . . ."

I glanced at Detective Cole; clearly Stanley was struggling with something. The detective nodded and gestured for me to walk a few feet away with him. When I did, he turned to me and explained, too quietly for Stanley to hear, "He's struggled, mentally, since Alice disappeared. His parents think he held himself responsible for what happened to her. He has a history of extreme anxiety, hearing voices. Been in and out of mental hospitals for the last ten years."

I sucked in a breath through my teeth. *Poor Stanley.* This case just seemed to provide more and more victims, from the kidnapped kids themselves, to their devastated parents and grandparents, to their shattered siblings. It was hard to understand who might be responsible for causing so much heartache.

"Okay," I said softly, nodding at Detective Cole. "Let's be as gentle as we can in our questioning, then."

We walked back to Stanley and sat down facing him. He was still babbling to himself, "I have to, I have to, I have to . . . ," while fidgeting in his lap.

"Stanley," said Detective Cole, "we're very close

to finding your sister. I really believe that. But we need your help. Can you tell me, why did you decide to come here, looking for Alice now? Is it because you saw Justin on the news?"

Stanley shook his head. "No," he said, "I don't even watch the news. It was because Alice finally contacted me, after all these years."

Detective Cole met my eye, and we exchanged surprised glances.

"How?" Detective Cole asked. "In your mind? Did you see her in a dream?"

Stanley shook his head. "No, nothing like that. I know the difference between Alice in my head and real Alice. She wrote me a letter that came in the mail."

Detective Cole frowned, clearly surprised. "What letter?" he asked. "Stanley, we've been holding you for days now, and we've searched through your things. There was no letter from Alice. Did you leave it at home?"

Stanley shook his head again. "It's safe now," he replied. "I had to hide it from the bad people. Alice says the bad people won't let her leave."

I glanced at the detective; that sure sounded accurate, if the little Frank had told us was to be believed. Alice was being held in the underground bunker by—well, we didn't know. But if she really had written to Stanley, maybe she had mentioned these "bad people."

Detective Cole furrowed his brows. "Where did you hide it, Stanley? You can tell us. It will help us find Alice."

Stanley looked skeptical. "I don't know," he replied. "I'm going to find Alice. I don't know if I can trust you. Alice needs me, her brother, not you."

The detective sighed. "She needs both of us, Stanley. I'm the police. When we find her, we need to punish the bad people who did this to her, and I can make that happen. Do you understand?"

Stanley frowned. He looked nervous, like he was not inclined to trust either one of us at all. I could tell he didn't understand what was going on here; he really thought he'd be walking out of the police station soon, able to resume his search for his sister.

"Can you tell us what the letter said?" I asked, wondering how a young girl imprisoned in an underground bunker had managed to stamp and mail a letter to her brother. Was Stanley lying to us? Or had Alice passed it to someone else? Did she have an ally in one of the bunker's staff members?

"It was very confusing," he replied. "She said

she missed me, and I had to come get her. Then she gave me some directions for finding where she is."

"Directions?" asked Detective Cole, eyebrows raised.

"That's right," said Stanley, nodding. "But I was having some trouble following them. So I buried the letter in the woods and went to try to find Justin."

"How did you know about Justin?" I asked quickly, though I could see Detective Cole was dying to get more information about where the letter was buried. "You said you don't watch the news. How did you know he was out, and could tell you where your sister was?"

Stanley chuckled, like the answer to my question was embarrassingly obvious. "Because he mailed the letter for her, silly," he replied. "She said he was going to escape, so she was giving him this message for me."

I looked at Detective Cole. So that was it: It sounded like the letter was real. From what Frank had told me, it seemed that Alice knew how to escape the bunker, probably because she'd seen Justin do it. And if she knew he was leaving, it made sense she would give him a message for her family. Within a couple of days of Justin's reappearance,

Stanley had shown up at the hospital, looking for him.

I glanced sideways at Stanley. "Does anyone know he's here?" I asked Detective Cole.

He nodded. "Of course. We called his parents this morning. They were thrilled to find out he's safe."

I tilted my head. "Did . . . um . . . *they* see the letter?" If a rational adult had laid eyes on whatever this letter said, maybe they had information about where Alice might be held, or whether the letter was even from her.

Detective Cole shook his head. "It seems Stanley brought in the mail that day," he replied. "And then promptly disappeared the next morning."

I looked back at Stanley. He was chewing on his fingernails now, staring off into the distance. If he realized we were talking about him, he gave no outward sign.

"Stanley," I said gently. "How come you didn't tell your folks about the letter? Wouldn't they help you find Alice? I'm sure they want to find her too."

Stanley's eyes came back into focus, and he looked at me like he had no idea why I was asking him that. His eyes watered. "Don't you see?" he asked, shaking his head. "Don't you?"

"See what?" asked Detective Cole, leaning in.

A tear trickled down Stanley's cheek, and he swiped at it angrily. "*I* was with her the day she disappeared. Alice. They took her from right beside me."

I took in a breath, trying to remember our research. He was right; Alice and Stanley had left their campsite on a hike five or six years before. Hours later, Stanley was found on the trail, knocked unconscious by someone or some*thing*. Alice was gone.

"I *lost* her," Stanley went on, more tears dripping from his eyes. "Don't you see? I had to be the one to get her back. If I get her back, my parents will forgive me and we can all be a family again."

I looked at Detective Cole, swallowing back a sympathetic sigh. *Poor Stanley.* He really believed he was responsible for Alice's disappearance. Meanwhile some psycho with a fondness for sedative drugs had taken her to—*what?* Keep her prisoner forever? Start a child army? Always have someone to watch *SpongeBob SquarePants* with? What?

Detective Cole touched Stanley's shoulder again. "Stanley, listen to me. We will get her back. You have to trust me on that. But the three of us working together can find her faster than you can. When your parents get here, we'll tell them you did it. We'll tell them you're the hero. But please—tell us where that letter is. Joe and I will go and dig it up and we'll find Alice as soon as we possibly can. You have my word on that."

Stanley was silent for a minute, wiping his cheeks with no expression. After a moment, though, he whispered, "Can I see her?"

"What?" I asked.

But he turned to Detective Cole. "When you find Alice," he explained. "Can I see her? Right away? I miss her a lot."

Detective Cole sucked in a breath and nodded slowly. "Of course, Stanley. You're the first person I'll bring her to. Okay?"

Stanley nodded slowly. "Okay," he said. Then he took a deep breath. "I buried the letter at our old campsite," he said, "by the river, under a tree that was broken in half."

I looked at Detective Cole.

"I know that tree," he said, nodding quickly. "I know all the crime scenes by heart, unfortunately. Where Alice and her family camped—there's a big old pine tree that got hit by lightning last year. That's where it's got to be."

Stanley nodded.

"Thank you, son," Detective Cole said, standing up and patting Stanley's arm. "You wait here, and we'll tell you as soon as we know anything, okay?"

"Okay," Stanley agreed. "Can I have a glass of milk, please?"

A few minutes later, as Detective Cole was explaining this break in the case to his fellow officers, and the receptionist was preparing a big glass of milk to bring to Stanley, my phone rang loudly. I jumped, then pulled it out and glanced at the caller ID.

MISTY FALLS HOSPITAL.

I smiled. *Good—so Frank's awake.*

"Hello," I answered, casually holding the phone to my ear as Detective Cole gestured for me to follow him out to the parking lot. We were headed for the state park—stat!

"Hello," said a nervous voice. "This is Nurse Appleby from the trauma ward at the hospital. To whom am I speaking?"

I frowned. "This is Joe Hardy, ma'am. Are you calling about my brother?"

There was a pause, and I thought I detected a little sigh on the other end. "Um, yes, I am, sir. See . . . the thing is . . . this really never happens here, but . . ."

My stomach clenched. *What happened to my brother?* Had he had a bad reaction to the sedative? Had his injuries worsened? "What?" I demanded.

The nurse sighed, more loudly this time. "The thing is," she said, "he's . . . missing."

On the Run

*T*hump. *Thump. Thump. Thump.* I blocked out all other sounds and thoughts as my feet slammed the pavement across the hospital parking lot and into the woods that led—I was pretty sure—in the direction of Misty Falls State Park. My heart pounded in my chest and my arm throbbed in its cast, but I couldn't slow down, and I *definitely* couldn't stop. I had to get away from hospital security, Dr. Carrini, and Chloe. Something big was going down in that underground bunker in the woods—something dangerous. Chloe knew what it was, and she'd chosen her secrets over me. That smarted a bit. But I was glad I'd learned the truth now, when I still had a chance at getting away.

Two security guards had followed me out the door, but I was smaller, younger, and faster than either of them. At first I could hear them close behind me, panting as their feet heavily slammed the ground. But as I crossed the lot, they'd grown farther and farther behind, until they were a good twenty yards behind as I crossed into the woods. One of them stopped at the border of the lot, hesitating.

"Jack?" he called to the second guard, who was still following me. "Is it worth it? He's off hospital property now."

The other guard paused, panting. "Maybe . . . maybe we should call the police."

I kept running. My feet pounded over dead leaves and exposed roots as I tore my own path through the dense woods. I could feel the chill of the forest air creeping up the back of my regrettably immodest hospital gown, but I didn't slow. As I ran, the edges of my vision went blurry, and occasionally dizziness caused me to veer or judge my distances wrong. The purple sedative, whatever it was Chloe had given me, was still affecting my brain. But adrenaline had given me enough clarity to make my escape.

Finally, what had to be a mile or more into the woods, I slowed.

I had to get to Joe. And I had no idea where he was right now. Worse, I had nothing on me—not my ATAC-issued phone, compass, or any sort of GPS device. If I showed my face in town, I would be dragged back to the hospital—not even Detective Cole could keep his officers from doing that. Best-case scenario, I'd end up in a tense standoff with Dr. Carrini and Chloe, where they insisted I was messed up on drugs and made up everything I was saying. I'd have Joe and Detective Cole to back up my story, but I knew it would take awhile to work everything out, anyway. And truthfully, even Joe and Detective Cole hadn't seen what I'd seen in that bunker. They couldn't imagine the weirdness. They could only trust that I was telling the truth.

So I had to get to Joe—and I had to stay out of sight. Which meant the best idea was probably to head back to our campsite in the state park. Hopefully it was still standing and hadn't been ravaged by bears or ghosts or whoever the heck had been tormenting us the last night I'd stayed there. I hadn't slept there in days, but Joe had still been in one piece this morning—whoever was responsible for the Misty Falls Lost hadn't gotten him yet.

I knew the park was northwest from the hospital, and within the park, our site was located on a river that ran through the eastern part (and, as we had found, was quite popular with bears). Looking up at the sun, I could see that it had already started its slow descent—to the west. Which meant that if I walked slightly to the right of the sun, I should be headed northwest, toward the park. It seemed a terribly inexact navigational system—especially for a guy half in love with the lady who narrated his GPS system in his car at home—but it was all I had. With one last stretch—and a quick adjustment of my hospital gown—I headed off to the right of the sun.

My stomach growled, and I thought of yet more stuff I didn't have: food and water. Of course, ATAC training included extensive wilderness survival training, so I knew how to find clean water—and if worse came to worst, I could survive on edible bark and roots. I hoped it wouldn't come to that, though. *I could really go for a burger,* I thought as I headed into the slowly setting sun.

I wasn't sure how long I had been walking, but according to the angle of the sun, it had been an hour or two since I'd left the security guards behind in the hospital parking lot. The park was about eight miles from the hospital, meaning I still probably had an hour or so to go. My mind had cleared a little as the drugs continued to wear off, and my vision was no longer blurry around the edges. I was having an easier time concentrating, too. I hoped I would be totally back to normal soon.

Still thirsty, I could hear a little rush of water over to my right, behind a copse of trees. I headed over to investigate and found a small, clear brook running over a rocky bed. After investigating, I decided that the water was safe to drink and leaned down by the shore, grabbing up full palmfuls and sucking them down with relish. Water had never tasted so good, or so clean, or cold! I sighed, enjoying the feeling of it sliding down my throat.

Crack.

I startled at a noise behind me. It sounded like a branch breaking. But surely that wasn't possible—out here? The forest was full of animals, but few would be big or powerful enough to snap a branch—few that came out during the day, anyway. The only explanation I could think of was that a human was following me.

Crack. Shuffle, shuffle.

Okay, there was no denying it now. My heart jumped into my throat as I realized the noise was coming from no more than a few yards away, and I was completely out in the open, by the brook with nowhere to hide. *Somebody* was coming. Could it just be a random hiker? The park was full of hikers and campers . . . being a state park and all. But with dismay, I reminded myself that I was miles from any sort of marked trail, and probably still a ways from the park boundaries. I was really still in the wilderness. There was no reason for someone to pass through here.

Except if they were looking for me.

How could anyone have found me, though? I had been careful as I was walking to double back a few times, create some false trails, and cover my tracks in case someone tried to track me through the woods. An experienced tracker could probably still find me, but would whoever was after me— whoever ran the murky whatever that was going on under the forest floor—have an experienced tracker? Nobody I'd encountered in the underground bunker had seemed like much of a woodsman. Definitely not Chloe.

I quickly ran my hand over my hospital gown, then fingered the hem and ran my hand up and under the inside. *There* it was—bingo! A tiny studlike device was attached at the seam, nearly undetectable. I grabbed it and pulled it out. It was small, round, and made of black plastic, with a metal center and a tiny blinking red light. *Has to be a GPS device,* I figured. If it was, then whoever had planted it could easily have been following me on a computer this whole time.

My heart sank. Who could have planted it on me? It had to be someone with access to the hospital. Chloe? One of the doctors? I shook my head. How far did this organization extend? Had I ever really had a chance at getting away? Could I still? I threw the device as far down the brook as I could and jumped to my feet. As someone crunched through the brush to reach the far side of the brook, I sprang into action, running as fast as I possibly could in the opposite direction.

My feet hammered the dry brush on the ground as I used all my ATAC wilderness training to forge a path through the dense woods. If I could outrun these guys, without the device on me, I still stood a chance of getting away. But I could hear footsteps hammering behind me—heavy, but fast. Whoever it was, I wasn't losing them. I started getting crazier with my movements, veering off at sharp turns, pounding through trees and scratchy branches. I could feel the sharp branches tearing into my skin, scratching me up, but I didn't care. I had to get to camp and to Joe!

I charged into a small clearing and stopped. To my left was a steep, craggy rock face, and to my right a small path led downhill through a bed of what looked like blackberry bushes. The path was the clear choice—and exactly where my pursuer would expect me to go, especially with my injuries. Instead I used my right hand to grab a shaky handhold up at my eye level on the rock face and tried to pull myself up. It was nearly impossible, but my training had given me enough arm strength to at least hold myself there for a few seconds, hanging against the rock, as I scrambled for a way to support myself with my left hand. I knew my left arm was too weak to support my weight, but my hand was free and could at least hold on to help balance myself. Maybe, if I was lucky, I could scramble up using mostly my right hand. Finally I found an outcropping to grab and shoved my bare feet into the rock, searching for something—anything!—to push myself up on.

I could hear footsteps approaching behind me. I had only seconds. Finally I found it—a tiny protrusion in the rock's surface, just big enough to get a couple of toes around, but it was enough. I molded my foot around it and pushed up, scrambling for and finding another handhold farther up the rock face. Then another, then another foothold, and finally I could reach up to the top of the ridge. I used my right hand to pull myself up and over, crying out as my left arm banged against the rock face. But it didn't matter. Within seconds, I was up at the top of the ridge, looking down as my pursuer reached the clearing.

A tall, stocky man walked into the clearing, wearing jeans and a sweatshirt. I bit back a gasp. *Baby Doc!* It was one of the "doctors" I'd seen in the underground bunker. He'd always seemed a little out of it—but he was definitely paying attention now. I watched as he looked around the clearing, frowning. He glanced at the rock face and up to the top—I ducked back behind some trees out of sight—and then he headed down the path between the blackberry bushes.

I took a deep breath. *Freedom!*

I waited a couple of minutes for Baby Doc to be out of earshot. Then I slowly backed away from the rocky drop-off. I wasn't sure where I was, but according to the sun, I was still facing west. Checking one last time to see that the clearing was empty, I turned to start my new hike—

—*and slammed right into Scar.*

"Where you going in such a hurry?" he said with a leer, grabbing me by the back of the neck and wrestling me to the floor with an athlete's precision. The scar that covered his face made me shiver, remembering my time in the bunker, how the kids had seemed to fear him. What was this? How had Baby Doc and Scar tracked me and found me? Why did they want me back so badly?

Just then footsteps approached from a line of sycamore trees. I gasped as Baby Doc emerged, talking on a cell phone. Had there been another way up here, around the rocky ridge? There had to be. Baby Doc wasn't even panting—like he'd just strolled up from wherever the blackberry path led.

"Yup, we got him," he told whoever was on the end of the line, then hung up. "Boy, are you going to be sorry you ran," he told me with a threatening grin.

What now? What could they do to me now? I admit it: My normally cool, calm exterior vanished, and I freaked out a little bit. "I won't go back to the hospital!" I cried, looking from one "doctor" to the other. "You can't take me against my will! I'm a free man!"

But Baby Doc just laughed. "Oh, we're way beyond that, kid. You've caused way too much trouble to go back to the hospital. No, you're going back underground."

And with that, they dragged me over the rocky ground a few yards away to what looked like a cave: a dark entrance leading into a craggy rock face, out of the bright sunlight. But as we walked a few yards in, a metal door opened.

We were heading back into the underground lab. And any chance I'd had of getting back to my brother was gone.

8

Memories

Detective Cole and I headed back to Misty Falls Hospital. We still wanted to check out that letter ASAP, but some things—like your sedated brother disappearing into thin air from a secure hospital—are more important than tracking down clues. As we drove, my stomach churned with worry over Frank. Why would he leave the hospital? My brother's a traditional guy—he trusts doctors, science, and the law. I couldn't imagine why he would have left the hospital without contacting me.

Unless he felt threatened.

Which led me back to the strange scene I'd witnessed this morning—Chloe sedating Frank and generally acting weird. She was usually so bubbly and friendly, but this morning she'd acted like she wished I'd take a long walk off a short pier. She'd seemed . . . nervous. I trusted her enough that I didn't think much of it at the time. But what if that nervousness had something to do with Frank bolting from the hospital? What if she, or the doctor, had tried to do something that Frank knew was dangerous?

"Don't worry, son," Detective Cole said with a weary sigh as he parked the police cruiser in front of the hospital entrance and patted my shoulder. "We'll get to the bottom of this, and we'll find your brother."

Inside, we asked after Frank at the nurse's station and were told to proceed to Dr. Carrini's office, where doctors were waiting to explain to us what happened. We followed the nurse upstairs to a quiet corridor of offices, where she led us into a large, bright corner office with DR. CARRINI scrawled on a Post-it note on the front door. Inside, Dr. Carrini stood with Chloe—*Chloe? So she* is *involved*—facing a huge window that overlooked the forest. When we strode in, Detective Cole cleared his throat, and Dr. Carrini and Chloe turned around, neither one looking super excited to see us.

"Well, hello," said Dr. Carrini, not quite meeting my eye. He glanced over at the nurse who'd led us up. "Thank you for bringing them up here, Nancy. I'm afraid we have some difficult things to discuss. You can go back to your duties."

"Of course, doctor," Nancy said with a nod, and with a sympathetic look at me, she headed back the way we'd come.

"Why am I meeting with you?" I asked bluntly, not wanting to waste any time. "When Frank was admitted, he was treated by a Dr. Klaus. What happened to him?"

Dr. Carrini sucked in a breath. "Please, sit down," he said, gesturing to two leather couches that faced an empty glass coffee table. "Forgive the impersonality of this office. It's temporary, you understand, and I haven't had much chance to decorate since I was called here to treat Justin."

"Why were you treating Frank Hardy?" Detective Cole repeated, remaining standing as I sat down. "Joe here asked you a question about his brother. Please answer."

Dr. Carrini nodded, shooting an uncomfortable smile my way. "I apologize. I see you're very concerned about your brother, and that's admirable." He took a seat on the couch facing me and gestured up at Detective Cole. "Please, sit down. Let's all be comfortable while we discuss some . . . uncomfortable topics."

Uncomfortable topics? If Dr. Carrini was hoping to calm me down, he was failing miserably right now. *Uncomfortable topics* implied that he was about to say something that would make me upset. And that was about the last sort of explanation I wanted.

"Joseph," Dr. Carrini began, and I stiffened at the use of my full name, which absolutely no one uses except teachers on the first day of school. "are you familiar with the claims your brother was making when he came in?"

I raised my eyebrows. "The claims he was making?" I asked, feeling an uncomfortable sense of déjà vu. "If you mean what he said about the underground bunker and the hatch . . ."

Before I could continue, Dr. Carrini leaped up and grabbed a folder from his desk, then opened it up and began to read off a paper. "'An underground bunker where he was held prisoner for several days,'" he said. "'No known entrance or exit. Subject claims a metal hatch led to a series of tunnels leading to the bunker, but said hatch was destroyed in an explosion, leaving no trail. Subject claims that the missing children whose disappearance he was investigating were *all* present in the bunker.'"

"That's not true," I broke in. "He didn't see all of them. But he thought—"

Dr. Carrini held up his hand. "He believed they might all be kept down there, is that correct?"

I tried to remember my conversation with my brother the night before. It felt like months ago. "Yes," I said finally. "I mean, it's possible. He saw a couple."

Dr. Carrini nodded sagely, like this was very important. "'Subject claims he and the other children were treated with drugs, making it impossible to remember anything clearly, or to be entirely certain about what he saw.'"

I frowned. I knew where this was going. "What does this have to do with where my brother is? I mean, isn't that the most important thing? Finding my brother?"

Dr. Carrini sighed, then nodded again. "You were asking why I took over your brother's care."

"That's right," I agreed.

He put down the folder, sat down on the couch again, and looked me in the eye. "I took over your brother's care because, as you saw with Justin, I am an expert in the science of memory—and the treatment of false memories."

I stared at him, my face growing hot as I

realized what he was saying. "You think my brother's *lying*?"

Dr. Carrini held up his hand, shaking his head. "Not lying," he countered. "I believe your brother thinks what he's saying is true. But that doesn't make his memories any more believable."

I glared at him, my temper getting the better of me. "Who are you to say what is and isn't believable?"

Dr. Carrini glanced at Chloe, who still looked deeply uncomfortable, then back at me. "Joseph, I am a reasonable human being. This is a quiet mountain town with a small population. Do you really expect anyone to believe that an underground bunker exists—and *has* existed all these years—filled with missing children being pumped full of drugs and I don't know what?"

I set my jaw in an angry line. "If my brother said it, yes."

"Very well," said Dr. Carrini. "He's your brother, and I hear you, Joseph, that he's usually a very trustworthy person." He paused, opening the folder again. "But there is still the matter of the drugs in his system. Five different drugs, when he was admitted to the ER, all of which could have effects on his judgment and ability to see things clearly."

I nodded. "He told me that. He told me they drugged him in—in wherever he was."

"Does your brother often use recreational drugs?" Dr. Carrini asked.

I snorted. "*Never.* We would never touch them. My brother barely ever takes an aspirin."

Dr. Carrini nodded. "So it's safe to say that introducing a large amount of drugs into his system very suddenly might have an extreme effect?"

I opened my mouth to reply, but stopped myself. *An extreme effect?* Frank had been acting weird the night before, sure. And definitely, crawling down into the rubble to save some girl only he could hear was weirdness in the extreme. Nothing like my cautious, by-the-book bro. But still, I just knew he wasn't making the whole thing up.

Didn't I?

Detective Cole cleared his throat. "The problem with that theory," he said, "is that Joe and I saw the hatch. A whole bunch of my men did, before it was blown up. So clearly Frank wasn't confused about *that.*"

Dr. Carrini turned to the detective with a patient, almost indulgent expression, like he was a little kid who'd just said something extremely cute. "We'll get to that," he said dismissively, then turned back to me. "Did you know, Joseph, that when your brother escaped from the hospital—in a very bizarre display of behavior, I must say—he attacked Chloe on the way out?"

Attacked Chloe? I shook my head. "That's impossible. That's not like Frank at all. He barely has the guts to *talk* to girls, much less . . ." I looked up at Chloe, who, I realized now, looked a little pale and shaken. She met my eye only briefly before looking down at the floor.

"It's true," she said quietly. "I couldn't believe it myself, because that's not like him at all. But he wasn't himself. He seemed very upset, like he'd had some kind of . . ."

"Mental break," Dr. Carrini supplied. "Perhaps drug-induced."

I frowned. I didn't like the direction of this conversation at all. "But *you* were the one pumping him full of drugs this morning," I insisted, looking at Chloe. "You were sedating him. Remember?"

Dr. Carrini leaned in. "And that's *all* we gave Frank," he insisted, "a sedative to help him sleep. Nothing that would cause hallucinations or the behavior we saw this morning, with him ripping out his IV, leaping out of bed, and running out of the hospital like a streak, attacking Chloe along the way. The drugs he had in his system when he arrived, however . . ."

I frowned. "But who *gave* him those drugs?" I asked, giving the doctor a challenging look. "If not you, if you don't believe the bunker exists, then who?"

Dr. Carrini leaned back. "I don't know," he said simply. "Perhaps someone who wants to impede the investigation. And it concerns me that they're succeeding."

Detective Cole frowned. "What's that supposed to mean?"

Dr. Carrini looked at him calmly, clearly not intimidated at all. "It means," he said, "that I have serious concerns about the direction of this investigation, based on what I observed with Justin and now with Frank. And I'm not the only one. Chloe, would you lead in our friends?"

Friends? I glanced at Detective Cole, but he looked just as surprised about all this as I felt. Chloe shot me a brief apologetic look. "Of course," she said quietly, then left the office.

We waited only a few seconds before I heard voices in the hall. Then Chloe led in a herd of people: Jacob, Donna, and Smith—no surprises there—but also Edie, Justin's mother, and Hank, her current husband. I looked at them, stunned. Jacob had been unpredictable and difficult since our investigation started, but Edie and Hank had always been reasonable and kind to Frank and me. Had they somehow been recruited into this stop-researching-the-bunker movement?

Edie, Donna, Hank ,and Jacob joined us on the couches, all looking a little uncomfortable. Smith went to stand by the window, looking at me with a smug expression.

"We have all," Dr. Carrini began, glancing around at them for confirmation, "been discussing the events of the last twenty-four hours. And we have serious concerns."

Jacob, Donna, and Smith all nodded enthusias-tically. I looked at Edie, waiting to see whether she was really part of this. She looked at me uncom-fortably—but then nodded. Then she looked down into her lap.

I heard Detective Cole take a deep breath. "What are your concerns?" he asked.

Jacob shrugged. "It's what we talked about this morning, detective. But we all agree. There's barely any evidence this bunker exists, much less that my kid is in it."

"And it's all . . . a little hard to believe," Hank added tentatively. "An underground bunker where kids are kept prisoner? Is this a better explanation for all the disappearances than bear attacks?"

"Besides," broke in Edie, looking apologetic,

"we all know your brother was drugged at the time he appeared in the woods—so why are we listening to him? Nothing he says makes any sense."

I glanced at Detective Cole and sighed. "I still believe my brother," I insisted. It was true, I didn't know who gave him the drugs he had in his system or exactly how they were affecting him—but I believed the essence of what he had told me.

Detective Cole nodded. "And I do as well."

"Well," Jacob said, "I think we're at an impasse here, folks. And I'm not going to sit here and watch you let my son get away while you investigate this cockamamie story. Neither are Edie and Hank."

I glanced at Edie and Hank; they looked uncomfortable but nodded slightly. "We have to find my boy," Edie whispered, her voice breaking.

"If you continue down this path, Detective Cole," Jacob went on, "I will have your job. That's a promise."

Detective Cole looked stunned, laughing nervously. "And how would you do that?" he asked. "Last I checked, I had the right to proceed with an investigation as I see fit. This is still the United States of America, isn't it?"

Jacob just gave him a dark look. "It is," he replied, "but the way the real world works is this. Donna has all kinds of connections to the Idaho government. You keep going this way, you'll be out—and that's for real."

My mouth dropped open as I looked at Detective Cole in shock. Jacob had always been difficult and less than cuddly—but impeding our investigation like this? Why?

SUSPECT PROFILE

Name: Jacob Greer

Hometown: Doddsville, Idaho, currently lives in Chicago

Physical description: 5'10", shaggy salt-and-pepper hair, brown eyes. A little heavy, rough around the edges.

Occupation: Sporting equipment salesman

Background: Justin's adoptive father; ex-husband of Edie; lives with his girlfriend, Donna; had distant relationship with Justin before he disappeared.

Suspicious behavior: Refuses to allow police to even investigate existence of an underground bunker where Justin may be held; hired his own PI to solve the case.

"You have got to be kidding me," Detective Cole went on, looking around the room at a series of hostile faces. "You would impede my investigation, right when we've had a break in the case? I saw the hatch with my own eyes."

"That may be true," Edie spoke up, her voice still wavering, "but only Frank really saw what was down here, and he's not the most trustworthy witness."

"Some of your men are going against you on this, too" Jacob added, glaring at Detective Cole. "Seems nobody but you is so sure they saw a hatch, or what that hatch was. Nobody's willing to testify about it in court, anyhow."

Detective Cole's mouth hung open in shock. I felt the same way. *His own men were with Jacob now?*

"I'll repeat," Jacob went on, "unless you change the course of the investigation, and send these troublemaking students back home," he added, glancing at me, "you will be out of a job by tomorrow morning. I told you, Donna has connections in the Idaho government; they can make things happen."

Detective Cole turned to Dr. Carrini, still looking shocked. "And you're okay with this?" he asked. "I'm basically being blackmailed to stop an investigation. You're a doctor, a man of science. You're okay with me not investigating every angle?"

Dr. Carrini looked Detective Cole right in the eye, unflinching. "I do think you should stop this line of investigation—for the health of everyone involved," he replied. "I am an expert in memory, after all, and I believe neither the 'memories' that Justin was having before he disappeared nor Frank's 'memories.' I believe both were false, or implanted, memories, and that means that someone is messing with these kids."

"Implanted memories?" I repeated. "What does that even mean?"

Dr. Carrini glanced at me impatiently. "We've

discussed this in regard to Justin. Someone suggests a memory to the patient, sometimes under the influence of drugs, and then reacts with excitement or approval when the patient appears to 'remember' it. You see cases of this with children who claim to remember their birth, or their christening, for example. In fact, their brains were not wired to *have* true memories at that age. But their parents have told them the story so many times, they believe they remember it as their own."

I thought that over. "But doesn't that mean . . . ?"

"Someone would have to have gotten to Frank and Justin to suggest these memories," Detective Cole filled in. "Who?"

Dr. Carrini shrugged. "I suppose that's the real question," he replied. "Your brother was missing for a long time, no? Who knows who he might have been in contact with in that time?"

I frowned. I didn't like this line of thought, but . . . still. I had to admit that Dr. Carrini was right about one thing: I really had no idea what had happened to Frank while he'd been gone. And I really had no idea why he'd left the hospital.

"Well," Detective Cole said after a few seconds, "you all don't frighten me. And you're certainly not going to stop me from doing my job. I owe this boy the courtesy of finding his brother and taking his claims seriously, and Edie and Jacob, I owe you the courtesy of finding your son— whether you believe in my investigation or not."

Jacob's eyes narrowed. "Well," he said after moment, "I'll see you fired, then."

Detective Cole stood, and I followed suit. "We'll see about that," promised the detective as the two of us strode out of the office.

ack Under

I tried to struggle, to get away from Scar and Baby Doc, but it was no use. These two had obviously had a lot of experience transporting people against their will. They held my arms like iron clamps as I was dragged down a series of dim tunnels, and back into the underground world I recognized. I tried to yell, "Help! Help me!" but Baby Doc's meaty hand clamped over my mouth before I could make more than a few pitiful sounds.

Baby Doc and Scar slammed through a swinging double metal door and shoved me into what looked like an operating room. Bright lights illuminated tile walls, medical equipment, and a couple of tables. My captors wrestled me down onto the table as tiny footsteps entered the room, and I heard a familiar voice.

"Frank! You're back!"

I struggled to see around the beefy orderlies. "Alice!"

She appeared just as I remembered her, dressed in a poufy pink princess dress with a little rhinestone tiara plopped on her messy blond head. She looked happy to see me. "You came back!" The fact that I was being wrestled onto a table by two orderlies didn't seem to faze her at all.

"Where's the purple stuff?" Baby Doc asked, opening a cabinet and looking at a series of IV bags. "We need to keep this one out of trouble for a while."

Alice's eyes opened wide. "No, no!" she cried. "You can't give Frank the Big Sleep . . . that's what happened the Bad Time! The time we lost—"

"Alice, go back to the playroom," Scar cut her off in an authoritative tone. "You know better than to mess with us when we're giving medicine. You know it's for his own good."

Alice looked doubtful, but at that point another young guy in scrubs appeared at the door. "Carl, take her away, please," Scar instructed. "Alice, Carl wants to play Princess Time with you."

Alice's face still showed doubt, but she allowed the third orderly to lead her out of the operating room. I looked around the room, trying to find anything I could grab and use as a weapon, when I spotted a body lying to my left and gasped.

Justin!

It was definitely him, lying unconscious on a gurney with an IV hooked up to his arm. Before I could react, though, Baby Doc rose over me again—this time with a clear bag of purple fluid clutched in his hand.

"If you know what's good for you, don't fight it," he told me as he handed the bag to Scar to hook up to my arm. "This is just to keep you out of trouble till the Big Boss can get down here."

The Big Boss? The Big Boss . . . As I mulled that over in my head, I felt Baby Doc remove the sheet I'd tied over my right elbow, and a needle jabbed painfully near where the other IV had been. I tried to struggle—to move my arm and throw them off—but it was no use. My left arm was throbbing in my cast, and already I could feel the warmth oozing through my veins. I struggled to keep my eyes open, but I was feeling drowsy . . . so drowsy . . .

Who knows how long later, I blinked awake, staring at the bright lights on the ceiling. I wasn't sure how long I lay there before I realized what was going on: I was awake! In the bunker! The operating room . . . I went to gasp, but a hand quickly clamped over my mouth. I let out a whimper of surprise, but then followed the hand up to the person standing over me.

Justin.

That's when I realized that Justin had disconnected my IV.

"Mmmmmff?" I asked him.

"Just relax," Justin whispered, looking sympathetic. "It's okay. They just gave you a little purple— not enough to give you the Big Sleep. It should wear off soon. You're going to be woozy for a while, but it will pass. I just need you to be quiet for a minute. The docs will be back any second now."

I took a deep breath and nodded. *Okay.*

Justin smiled. "Man, I've become a total expert on disconnecting IVs in this place. You take it off and then play dead, and the docs never figure out you're conscious. That's how I escaped the first time, and I still don't think they've caught on. Not the sharpest knives in the drawer, down here. They think if they give you enough drugs, they can totally control you."

I nodded again.

"Before I escaped," Justin went on, "that's how

I got in trouble. I was getting older, you know, and starting to remember what life was like with my parents before I got down here. I started asking too many questions, challenging the doctors too much." He scowled. "That's when they start drugging you to keep you out of their hair. They gave me so much purple, I was messed up for days—even once I got to the hospital. But even while they were drugging me, I knew I had to get out. Because they'll give you too much and your heart will just stop. That's what happened to Sarah."

Sarah? I remembered—the one of the Misty Falls Lost whose remains had been found in an abandoned bear cave. For years those remains had given credence to the idea that the disappearances had been due to bear attacks and other natural accidents. But was Justin—and Alice, she'd said something before about the "Bad Time"—were they saying that Sarah had been killed accidentally? Given too many drugs, then placed out in the wilderness to throw off the investigation?

I had so many questions. What *was* this place? How and why did Justin escape? Did all of the Misty Falls Lost end up here? But before I could get through even one—before I could even convince Justin to lift up his hand and let me talk—he cocked his head, listening. Then he quickly plugged my IV back in. I let out a shout of protest, but Justin shook his head at me.

"They're coming," he hissed, then dove back to his own gurney, reattaching his IV and playing dead.

I closed my eyes and heard heavy footsteps enter the room.

"Well, you're in big trouble now," says Baby Doc. "The Big Boss is coming—and he's not happy."

Map Quest

D etective Cole and I stood in the parking lot of Misty Falls Hospital, both shaken. I felt like neither one of us knew quite what to say after that meeting.

"Listen," I said finally. "If you want to back off the investigation—to save your job or whatever—I totally understand. I won't leave Misty Falls until I find Frank and get some answers, but there's no reason you should lose your job over it."

Detective Cole just snorted. "Forget it, kid," he said defiantly. "I've worked for the Misty Falls PD for almost thirty years, and done a damn fine job of it, except for finding these kids. I'm not about to lose this job, or be kept from finally finding them, over some deadbeat dad's guilt. I don't know what Jacob's problem is, but he's wrong. Dead wrong. Now let's go find that letter."

Well, all righty then. We hopped into the police cruiser and drove to the park, then hiked up from the parking lot to the site where Stanley, Alice, and their family had camped. It felt strange being back in the park. The last time I'd seen this campsite had been with Frank, when Farley, the now deceased crusty park ranger, had been giving us a tour to support his theory that the disappearances were all natural. Of course, that had been before we realized that Farley was Justin's biological grandfather, and before Farley had been savagely murdered in his own cabin. So much had happened since Frank and I had arrived on the scene. One thing was for sure: This was bigger than a few random bear attacks.

"Here," said Detective Cole, pointing to a tree that had been broken in half, probably by lightning. "It must be under here."

Sure enough, we found a little mound of loose black dirt right near the tree's base. Detective Cole started gingerly digging with his fingers, and before long he pulled out a bright pink piece of ruled paper, filled with colorful writing and drawings in multicolored marker. He unfolded it, and we both looked down.

"Help me, Lee," the letter started out, in the childish handwriting of a ten-year-old. "I need you."

They keep us here and they call it Happyland. We have lots of toys and we get to play all day. The grown-ups here are fun, not like normal grown-ups, and they like to pretend and help us use our imaginations.

But yesterday I asked about Mommy and Daddy, and where you are and when I would see you again. Today they gave me purple and made me sleep for three hours. They said I need to relax and stop worrying about things that don't really matter. They give my friend Justin the purple too, and I'm worried because I don't want him to get the Big Sleep. Justin says he's going to leave this place, so I'm giving him this letter to give you.

*Please come get me, Lee. I
don't want to stay in Happyland
anymore. I want to live with you
and Mommy and Daddy and go to
school and wear normal clothes.
When I say that to grown-ups
here, they say that's not being a
kid, being a kid means getting to
live in a world of imagination. But
I miss you. Here is a map to the
bunker. Please come get me, Lee.*

Underneath were some crude drawings, that looked like the piles of rocks Detective Cole and I had noticed earlier that we thought might have some role in leading people to the bunker entrances. I tried to make sense of Alice's drawings, but I couldn't. They were the drawings of a young girl—and worse, a young girl who hadn't been aboveground in years now. Still, I couldn't help thinking that this letter included some good information. The piles of rocks were carefully colored and drawn. If I could compare them against another map—a more reliable map—maybe we could find our way to an entrance?

That's when I remembered: the notes I'd seen

on Farley's calendar! When we found Farley's body, I'd noticed some interesting notes he'd made on the calendar on his desk, but the handwriting had been so chicken-scratchy, I couldn't make it out. I'd taken photos and sent them off to ATAC headquarters to be decoded. I'd been so distracted the last couple of days, I hadn't finished reading the analysis from ATAC. I grabbed my phone from my pocket and checked my e-mail—and there they were, waiting for me! Translated notes from ATAC.

See area A4 on map—pile of stones on right—entrance believed to be in vicinity . . .

"I think I've got something," I told Detective Cole.

"What's that?"

I showed him my phone, the e-mail containing the translated notes. "Notes I found on Farley's calendar last time I was there. The handwriting was so bad, I couldn't make them out. I had to send them to ATAC to be translated."

Detective Cole frowned. "See area A4 on map . . . what map?"

I nodded. "Exactly. Sounds like Farley must have had a map we never came across."

Detective Cole nodded slowly. "And maybe if we compared that map to this letter, we'd come up with something."

I nodded again. "Couldn't hurt."

Without another word, we hiked back to the cruiser and headed for Farley's cabin. It still stood empty. I had a feeling the state park was going to have a hard time recruiting rangers considering what had happened to Farley and another park ranger, Bailey, who'd been killed by a rattlesnake just days after Farley was found. Something rotten was definitely going down at this park, and I didn't care what Jacob said—something as crazy as what my brother had been suggesting was the only thing crazy *enough* to explain everything that had happened.

"Here we are." Detective Cole pulled into Farley's driveway and cut the engine. Without another word, we glanced at each other and got out, climbing up the stairs and under the police tape to enter the house.

The cabin was deadly silent inside, and it gave me the willies. It's hard to describe, but it felt like someone—or some*thing*—was inside, watching us, or had just been inside. I still had trouble believing that Farley had been killed here just days ago. I remembered how freaked I was when we first arrived at camp—terrified by the weird noises at night, sure that something ghostly was after us. Now those fears seemed almost cute compared to what was really going on. Murders, drugged kids, underground labs—I had never imagined that such crazy stuff could happen in the wilds of Idaho!

Detective Cole and I split up: He searched the downstairs, I searched the upstairs. The cabin had been searched for evidence after Farley's death, of course, so little of note remained. I looked everywhere: closets, under the bed, behind the furniture, even in the tank of the toilet. Anywhere the police might have missed. But after an hour of searching, I'd come up with nothing.

"You finding anything?" I called to Detective Cole.

He took a minute to answer. "Um . . . not exactly," he said finally. "Not what I was looking for, but . . . why don't you come on down?"

Hmmm. I quickly descended the stairs and found the detective standing in the living room.

"Look there," he said, pointing at the couch. It looked exactly like it had the last time we were there . . . *except.*

"Did you move the pillow?" I asked. A handsewn pillow had been thrown to the floor by the end table.

"Nope," said Detective Cole. "But it wasn't there before, right?"

I shook my head. "It was definitely on the couch. Are you sure . . . ?"

He raised an eyebrow. "This isn't the only thing I've noticed out of place since we got here. I'm pretty sure the shades in the study were down when we last left the cabin; now they're up. And I think Farley's files have been searched. There were files out of order and papers misfiled."

Hmmm. I looked at Detective Cole. "You sure Farley wasn't just a bad filer?"

He nodded. "I also found this on Farley's desk." He picked up a tiny item from the coffee table and handed it to me. I squinted: It was a hair.

A short hair, probably male in origin.

A distinctive chestnut brown, as though recently dyed.

My eyes widened as it came to me. "Smith," I whispered.

"It looks like his hair color, doesn't it?" asked the detective. "And about the right length and texture?"

I nodded. "Definitely."

Detective Cole frowned. "When I unlocked the door, I noticed that the safety lock hadn't been put on. I couldn't imagine my men letting that slide. But Smith . . ."

I nodded. "You think he's been prowling around here?" I asked.

Detective Cole sighed. "Seems that way."

"But why?"

He shrugged. "Who knows? To get evidence he or Jacob thinks we're missing? To slowly drive us insane? I don't know and I don't care. All I know is, he's disturbing a crime scene—and that's illegal."

He pulled out his cell phone and dialed. "Yeah, Casey. Get me Officer Dunham. I need you to bring in Michael Smith, Jacob Greer's PI, for questioning."

I waited while he explained the situation to one of his men. When he finished, he hung up and looked around the room. "I wish we'd found something. But if Smith was in here, maybe he beat us to the map?"

"Maybe." I shrugged. "But he doesn't even believe the bunker exists, does he? Why would he need a map to a place he doesn't believe in?"

Right then, Detective Cole's phone rang. "Cole here," he answered. He paused while he listened to the officer on the other end of the line, then sighed. "You're kidding me." He shook his head. "He's lying. I know he is. There's something going on with those two. Something they're not telling us." He listened to the caller again. "All right. But put out the word that there's a warrant to bring him in. And tell all the men to keep an eye out. Thanks."

I watched his face as the detective hung up the phone. "They found Jacob at his hotel," he explained, "but Smith isn't with him. He isn't in his room, either. Jacob says he has no idea where the guy is—he was supposed to be taking a nap."

"You don't believe that?" I guessed.

"Do you?" Detective Cole asked. "Seems a little convenient, doesn't it? But that's all right. My men will find him eventually."

I nodded, looking around the room. "Well, I hope they find him. And I hope he has the map Farley referred to. Because right now, I don't have any idea where it could be."

Detective Cole looked thoughtful. "Where would a guy like Farley hide something?"

I shrugged. "On his knife? With his compass? He was such a survivalist kind of guy."

"Yeah," Detective Cole agreed, "but both of those things are at the station with the rest of the evidence. And nobody saw anything unusual among the things they took."

I frowned. "Well . . . I'm stumped. Should we take one more look around before we go?"

Detective Cole shrugged. "Couldn't hurt."

He walked out into the kitchen, and I headed to the left, into Farley's study. Most of Farley's important papers had been kept in here . . . but they had also been searched by Cole's men, who'd found nothing unusual. Little remained in Farley's desk, and what was there was mostly harmless: pens, paper, Post-it notes. The bookshelf held just a few wilderness guides and a few framed pictures. I walked over and picked up one of the guides, flipping through the pages.

> One survival technique upon spotting a bear
> is to sing. The singing alerts the bear that
> you are human and thus not a threat. . . .

I looked up at the framed photos. Many of them were of Farley alone, on some sort of travels— Farley on a small boat. Farley on a mountain. Farley beside a waterfall. There were also a couple of Farley with his late wife, birthday- or anniversary-type poses. But . . .

Then I saw it.

It was a small picture, old and a little faded, in a tiny silver frame. Farley posed with a young boy, holding up fishing poles and smiling widely. I looked closer at the boy and gasped: It was Justin! He had to be only about three or four years old in the photo. Even Farley looked young and optimistic. I looked closer and noticed some paper sticking out of the side of the frame, like there was something in there behind the photo. I removed the photo from the frame and pulled out a folded piece of white paper. Opening it up, I smiled: It was a hand-drawn map of what appeared to be part of the park, including the campsites where kids had been taken. Was it possible? Had Farley had some sense that the underground bunker existed before he died?

That's when I noticed a hand-scrawled note at the top of the map:

I AM BEING WATCHED. IF YOU
FIND THIS AND SOMETHING
HAS HAPPENED TO ME, IT
IS BECAUSE OF THIS MAP—
AND BECAUSE I AM CLOSE TO
FINDING THE TRUTH.

This was it. "Detective Cole!" I called. "I found it! The map! It's unbelievable! Detective Cole!"

I paused, and heard nothing in reply. I frowned. Had he stepped outside?

"Detective?" I called again.

Nothing. I didn't even hear anybody moving.

I could feel the little hairs on the back of my neck standing up. Something felt wrong—very wrong.

"Detective Cole?" I ran through the living room to the kitchen now. "Detective Cole?"

Some of the contents of the cabinets were disturbed, like Detective Cole had been searching through them—but there was no sign of him.

"Detective Cole?" I called.

I ran outside. The cruiser was still parked in the driveway, undisturbed. "Detective Cole? Detective Cole!" I started shouting now, running around the yard. I ran all around the cabin, shouting, but there was no sign of him. Then I ran back into the cabin, doing a quick search of the upstairs, then the downstairs, but there was nothing.

It was like he had never been there.

A cold fear gripped my stomach.

Detective Cole was missing!

Motives Unknown

I braced myself to meet the Big Boss. Who could it be? Who would possibly run this kind of operation? But when the operating room doors opened and a figure rushed in, I didn't expect to see—

"Chloe??"

She frowned at me, suddenly looking very cold and businesslike. "That was a stupid stunt you tried today," she announced brusquely. "Did you really think you'd get away with it? Did you think we'd let you go?"

Confused, I just stared at her for a moment. "I—I—" I didn't know what to say. Why was Chloe acting like this? Who was she, really?

Chloe shook her head. "You've really done yourself in, Frank. He'll be here any minute, and I don't know what he's going to do. You need to be controlled."

My blood ran cold. *Controlled?* That didn't sound like they were going to drug me up and feed me sandwiches. It sounded a lot more painful, in fact. Just then, Alice burst through the door and came running up to Chloe.

"Chloe, Chloe!" she called. "Yay, you came today! Let me show you . . ."

I expected Chloe to brush the girl off, but instead her demeanor completely changed. She brightened and her eyes warmed, and she looked down at Alice with excitement. "Oh, Alice! How wonderful! What beautiful thing have you made for me?"

Alice held up some pink, fluffy, fairylike thing. "I made it in the Creativity Room," she said proudly.

"Oh, it's beautiful," gushed Chloe. "Can you tell me a story about it? What do you do with it?"

Alice screwed up her face. "Um, I guess . . . you can use it to clean your room? Like if your mommy asks you?

Chloe's face darkened, and she gently shook her head. "No, Alice. You only have to use it for play.

We're all children here." She rubbed Alice's head gently, and Alice, looking only a little disappointed at Chloe's answer, looked up at me.

"Is Frank going to be okay?" she asked.

Chloe smiled. "Don't you worry," she told Alice. "Frank's going to get what he deserves."

Watching this, my blood chilled. Chloe had completely changed personalities in a matter of seconds. And her dedication to this place—whatever this place was—clearly outranked any feelings she had for me or anyone else. I wondered, for just a moment, whether Chloe could be behind this whole thing. Could she be the Big Boss? I'd always heard Big Boss referred to as "he", but still . . .

SUSPECT PROFILE

Name: Chloe Evans

Hometown: Misty Falls, Idaho

Physical description: 5'5", shoulder-length black hair, blue eyes. Pretty.

Occupation: Candy striper, student, official in some sort of underground bunker prison

Background: Unknown.

Alice looked at me for just a second more before running off down the hall. Chloe stared after her fondly.

"Chloe," I said when she was gone, "what goes on down here, really? Please tell me. You can tell me the truth. I can see it's important to you."

Chloe turned and looked at me again, her expression thoughtful. I could tell she was debating how much to tell me. Finally she sighed. "Well, all right. You're not going to be around much longer anyway; I guess I can tell you."

Not going to be around much longer? I tried to block out that chilling statement and listen to the rest of what Chloe was telling me.

She cleared her throat. "This," she said, "is Happyland."

"Happyland?" I croaked. "It seems more like a laboratory."

Chloe nodded. "Well, it is, in a way. Happyland is a facility dedicated to raising children in the most age-appropriate, happy, and stress-free way possible. And yes, before you ask, all of the Misty Falls Lost were here at one point."

I gasped. But Chloe rushed on: "And they're better off for it! All you know about these kids is the news stories, how their parents missed them *sooo* much and were *sooo* sad. But what kind of parents were they really to these children? They fought; they got divorces; they argued about money and housing and work. In the real world, parents impose their worries on their kids; here, the children are free to just be children!"

"Except when they're drugged," I pointed out dryly. I could still feel the "purple" slowing down my reflexes.

Chloe made a face. "Oh, you're one of *those,* are you?"

"One of what?" I asked.

Chloe sneered. "The new agey, antidrug brigade. Sometimes drugs are good for children, Frank! What is a drug but a chemical that makes you feel better? And childhood is hard; there are disappointments and confusions. Sometimes these kids have memories from their less-than-perfect family lives, and a little dose of sedative helps them deal with those fears and worries! And it also helps them . . . to forget." She paused, pulling her mouth into a tight line.

Even under the effects of the "purple," my heart was pounding at the craziness of what Chloe was spouting. It was okay to take children away from their parents if their parents weren't perfect? It was good for those children to forget those parents? *But why did they need to forget? Why were they afraid and worried? Why were all bad emotions banished in this place, even if the only alternative was to feel nothing at all?*

Before I could speak again, though, there was a commotion in the hallway. The operating room doors swung open, and suddenly Baby Doc and Scar were struggling to bring in the comatose body of a large adult.

"Oh, good," said Chloe, looking completely unsurprised by this development. "You got him. What about the other?"

Baby Doc sighed. "Well, we tried, but he, um, he had his phone in his hand—it didn't seem safe to go after him. Besides, we got the important one."

Chloe glared at him, clearly furious. "The *other* one was more important! My God, we have his brother! Do you really think he's going to let that go?"

Baby Doc didn't answer as he and Scar laid the body on the gurney next to mine. As they rolled it over, I gasped and recognized him: Detective Cole.

Before I could react, though, a familiar voice boomed in the hallway. "Are they here? Did you get them all?"

A figure burst through the door, glaring right at me.

My mouth dropped open.

It was Dr. Carrini.

Bear Habitat

Twenty minutes after I first realized Detective Cole was missing, I was still standing in Farley's study, unsure what to do with myself. I hadn't heard anyone approach the cabin, or any kind of struggle. Was it possible Detective Cole had left of his own accord? I even considered: Was it possible he was somehow involved in the bunker, or had turned on me?

SUSPECT PROFILE

Name: Detective Richard Cole

Hometown: Misty Falls, Idaho

Physical description: 6'2", 245 pounds, 48 years old, thinning brown hair, hazel eyes. stocky.

It didn't take me long to realize that was nuts. Just the crazy wonderings of a freaked-out, desperate ATAC agent who *still* hadn't found his brother and had now lost his only friend. The truth was, I had no idea how to proceed. I hardly ever worked alone. And now, with the maps spread out in front of me on Farley's desk, I was so close, and yet so far.

I was freaked for another reason too. If Cole had really been *taken*—if he'd left against his will—then that meant someone had come here, to the cabin, undetected. Farley had known he was in danger—someone was after him, probably the same person who was after me, my brother, and Cole. And if they took Cole, they had to know I was here too. Were they still outside, lurking, waiting for their chance to grab me? I reminded myself that I'd run around the whole perimeter of the cabin, alone, looking for Cole—that would have been an ideal time to grab me. But I had no idea who these people were, or what their motives might be.

With a sigh, I picked up my phone and called the Misty Falls PD.

"Misty Falls Police Department, Casey speaking."

I took a deep breath. "Hi Casey. This is Joe Hardy, the student who's been working with Detective Cole. I have some . . . um . . . disturbing news."

"What's that?" Casey sounded a little wary.

"Well . . . I'm afraid he's missing."

"*Missing?* Detective Cole?"

"That's right. We were searching Farley's cabin for clues, and when I went to look for him, he was gone. I've searched the whole cabin, and the perimeter of the property, but there's no sign of him. I'm afraid he was abducted."

Casey let out a breath. "Are you sure he didn't just leave on his own?"

"Yes. His cruiser is still here, and all his stuff. He wouldn't just leave me like that, I'm sure of it."

There was a pause as he seemed to take that in.

"All right. We'll send out a team immediately. In the meantime, don't move, and don't touch anything."

Click.

I pushed the end button on my phone. Well, it was official: I was persona non grata with the Misty Falls PD. No big surprise really, since things had started getting really weird with this case ever since my brother and I had showed up to do "research." And now with many of Cole's men turning against him, claiming they weren't sure the hatch was what he thought it was, I was sure they saw me as a bad influence on their man. Now I'd gone and lost him. I was a troublemaker extraordinaire in their eyes.

I turned back to Farley's map and Alice's letter. They were laid out side by side on the desk. Each document was missing pertinent information, which was probably why Farley had never located the bunker and Alice—well—Alice was just a young kid. Still, taken together, they seemed to tell a story. Alice's drawing showed two rock piles north of the broken tree by her campsite and close to what looked to be a cave—the entrance to the bunker, I was pretty sure. But the distances were all off. Frank and I had been to that part of the park, and there had been no cave that close by. I had no doubt that Alice knew these landmarks, but it seemed she was missing some directional details.

Farley, on the other hand, had a comprehensive map that included topography, pertinent landmarks, even little notations about deer habitats and beaver dam locations. But he'd clearly still been trying to figure out what the rock piles led to, because there were questions scrawled in various locations, like *Entrance here? Cave looks recently disturbed—part of plan? Could they be underground?*

Frowning, I looked from one drawing to the other. Farley had a rock pile just north of Alice and Stanley's campsite too, but he didn't have a second rock pile, and he had a cave noted on the west side of the park—on the wrong side of the river to be Alice's cave/entrance. So where could the entrance be? I stared at Farley's careful drawings and notations. How close had he been to finding the truth? And how different might this case have turned out, how many lives saved, including his own, if he had just had a little more info?

That's when I saw it. *Bear Habitat*. The words were scrawled over a little circle by the river—close to, if a good bit east from, where Alice had drawn the entrance. I knew from Farley (and a host of cartoons) that bears liked to hibernate in caves. And the little abducted girl whose remains had been found, who they insisted was attacked by bears—her remains had been found in an abandoned bear cave.

Could that cave be the very entrance to the underground bunker?

My heart sped up. I knew I was onto something. According to the map, the cave was about a fifteen-minute hike from Farley's cabin; I could be there before it got dark. I frowned, glancing to the driveway, where there was no sign of visitors. Should I wait for the police?

I stood up, feeling restless and edgy. Something in my gut was telling me this was *right*. With Farley and Alice's help, I was closer to finding the bunker than ever. And more than that, I just *knew* my brother was down there. If he were free, Frank would have found his way to me by now. And Frank was a professional agent, like me. It would take a seriously organized operation to hold him hostage. Otherwise, we'd been extensively trained in negotiation and escape. Frank could have gotten away—if it were possible to get away.

Then there were Jacob, Smith, and the situation at the hospital. Everyone had been acting squirrelly—trying to make us believe Frank was out of his mind rather than telling the crazy truth. It seemed like they had some motivation to keep us from finding Frank, whatever it might be. And they all had access to him at the hospital. They might have easily taken him back to the bunker, if they were involved in the bunker in the first place.

I sighed, grabbing the maps. I knew what I had to do. I had to go save my brother.

I folded the maps, shoving them into my pocket, and looked outside. Already the light was fading and this long day was ending. It would be dark before long. And . . . I swallowed. I couldn't really go alone, could I? From the way Frank described it, there was a whole staff down there. And whoever was running the place wouldn't take kindly to visitors. I sighed again, feeling desperate, and redialed the Misty Falls PD.

"Misty Falls Police Department, Casey speaking."

"Hi, Casey. This is Joe Hardy. I just called."

"Yes." There was a pause. "Did you find Detective Cole after all?"

I let out a breath. "No. Listen. Change of plans. I am entirely sure that I know where my brother and Detective Cole are being held, okay? I need backup to meet me at the following location." Looking at Farley's map, I did my best to describe the location of the "Bear Habitat." "It's where the young girl's remains were found—the only member of the Misty Falls Lost to turn up. You remember?"

"Of course I remember," Casey said. "Sarah Finnegan. That was a very sad day for all of us, Mr. Hardy. But what makes you think your brother and Detective Cole are being held there? It's an abandoned cave."

I frowned. "Look—it would take too long to explain, and we're losing light. I need you to trust me. Please."

Casey waited a moment before responding. "Most of my officers were just sent to Farley's to look for Cole. Which is more important?"

I sighed. "This is. Please. If it turns out to be nothing, they can be back at Farley's cabin in minutes, no harm done."

There was another pause. "I'm sending one pair of officers to the cabin, and the rest to meet you. I want to make sure you haven't disturbed the crime scene at Farley's."

I felt a rush of relief. "Great. Thank you. When can they be at the cave?"

"Give them half an hour."

Click.

This time, the hang-up didn't bother me. I put the phone into my pocket with a smile on my face.

I just knew I was about to solve this thing.

After about ten minutes of fast hiking, I arrived at the entrance to a cave. On the way, I'd passed a pile of rocks that hadn't been on Farley's map— that must have been the second pile Alice drew! Which made me even more sure that this was the entrance to the bunker. Once I reached the cave, though, I realized that it was nearly dark. In fact, in the silent dusk, as I waited for the officers, the night seemed to get even *darker* in a matter of minutes. Cricket chirps filled the air, and the occasional flutter of animal tracks through the trees. I gulped, thinking back to my first days with Frank at our campsite—how every flutter and noise had seemed dangerous. And in the end, it had turned out to *be* dangerous. For all of Frank's teasing about my paranoia, he'd been the one abducted from the site in the early hours of the morning.

Something evil was lurking in these woods, for sure. And it sure as heck wasn't bears.

That's when I heard a *snap* behind me—like something (or someone) big stepping on a branch. Was it the police? But it sounded like someone trying to be quiet. . . .

"Hello?" I called, hoping to spot a cluster of officers. "Hello?"

No answer.

I frowned, taking a breath to calm myself down. *You're expecting people,* I reminded myself. *Besides, it was probably just a deer or an elk.* I pulled out Farley's map to study it again. *Bear Habitat . . .* but the cave had been abandoned for years, right? So there was no reason to worry—

I let out a cry as suddenly someone grabbed me from behind, and I felt the cold, sharp steel of a knife being held to my neck!

"Are you with them?" a voice demanded. A familiar, somewhat crazy voice. Trying to protect my throat, I carefully turned to look at my attacker and gasped.

It was *Smith*—Jacob's PI!

Just Keep Him Talking

"*You*," Dr. Carrini growled, looking at me with piercing, cold eyes. He'd never been a warm and fuzzy guy, but now he looked steely. "You couldn't just stay put, could you? I was going to keep you in the hospital as long as I could, keep you sedated, try to confuse you and convince you that you hadn't seen what you thought you had. But *noooo*. You had to play the hero. Well, you're going to suffer for it."

I squirmed on the gurney, feeling more vulnerable than ever. "Suffer?" I asked, and it came out squeakier than I intended. I wanted to keep him talking—an ATAC agent knows that a talking criminal is too busy to commit a crime—but I was also starting to fear for my safety, honestly. This was all getting really weird, really fast.

Dr. Carrini sneered at me. "That's right, I'm afraid. I'm not a violent man, Frank. In all my years of running Happyland, I've never intentionally hurt anyone. I've managed to keep my operation secret, and let the useless investigators believe that the children disappeared naturally. But then you and your brother showed up, and all hell broke loose."

I winced. "Well, to be fair, it really all started getting crazy when Justin escaped."

Dr. Carrini glared at me. I could see that I'd one-upped him, and he knew it, and it made me bolder.

"And he escaped," I said, "because you wouldn't answer his questions, and you started giving him high doses of drugs. You lied just now when you said you never hurt anyone. You killed little Sarah Finnegan by giving her a high dose of sedatives, and then you dumped her body in a bear cave to throw off the investigators."

Dr. Carrini continued to glare at me, his right eye twitching slightly. "I said I never *intentionally* hurt anyone. As everyone here will tell you, Sarah's death was an accident."

Seeing I'd hit a vein, I kept going. "An unnecessary accident. What kind of doctor messes up the dosing of a sedative? Are you even a real doctor?"

His eyes flashed. "Am I a *real doctor?*" he repeated, incredulous.

Chloe, who'd been watching our exchange with concern—concern for Dr. Carrini, not me, as far as I could tell—broke in. "Of course Dr. Carrini is a *real doctor*," she insisted, glaring at me like she was disciplining a naughty child. "He's one of the foremost experts on memory in the country."

"That's right," Dr. Carrini said. "My research has changed the entire thinking on how memories are formed, kept, and controlled."

"Controlled?" I asked. "Like you were going to control my memories of being in the bunker? Like you control these kids' memories of their parents by drugging them and confusing them?"

His eyes narrowed. Chloe shook her head, like she was dismayed that I just couldn't understand.

"What *is* this place, anyway?" I asked. "Why did you create it? Why have you been stealing other people's children?"

Dr. Carrini let out a big sigh. He glanced at Chloe, who shrugged.

"I suppose I can tell you," he said, regaining some of his composure and fixing me with the same calm, condescending stare I remembered from the hospital. "Since you're not going to be around much longer."

A chill ran up my spine, but I ignored it. *Keep him talking,* I told myself. *Just keep him talking, and hope that something changes.*

"Start at the beginning," I said, looking around. "What is this place? What gave you the idea?"

He smiled. "'This place,' as you so elegantly call it, is an extensive nuclear bomb shelter that was built by an eccentric, wealthy park ranger in the 1960s."

I frowned. "How come nobody knows about it?"

"I said the ranger was eccentric," Dr. Carrini said. "He simply didn't tell anybody, he paid the builders for their silence, and he confined the bunker to the most remote areas of the park, where the construction was unlikely to be noticed off-season."

Weird. "How did you find out?"

"This gentleman came under my care late in his life," Dr. Carrini replied. "Alzheimer's. I was completing my residency in Boise. He told me these remarkable stories about the bunker, which I assumed—and I told his family—were false memories, the result of dementia. But then, one weekend, I just had to see for myself. And sure enough, it was all here, just as he'd described."

Really, super weird. "So you decided to use it to build . . . Happyland?"

Dr. Carrini shook his head. "It was years before the idea for Happyland occurred to me. As I established myself as a memory expert, I saw it over and over again: children troubled by things they'd witnessed early in life. Parents fighting over money, arguments they were too young to process."

"Is that what happened to you?" I asked. "Did bad memories from childhood haunt you, too?"

Dr. Carrini looked angry, but then his expression softened. "I suppose you could say that," he admitted finally. "My mother died when I was young, and my father was cold and distant. He made me do extensive chores around the house, and when I was just twelve, I began working outside the house to earn my keep. My father seemed to view me as free labor, not as a child to be loved. I couldn't help feeling I'd missed out on my childhood." He paused. "But then, don't most children miss out on a true childhood?"

I leaned closer. "What do you mean?"

Dr. Carrini huffed. "In this modern world, parents are too concerned with their own lives— their complicated relationships, their guilt, their stress, and their money worries. That's what I've witnessed in my practice. They push that stress onto their children, who never get to experience being truly young and carefree. *Except* in Happyland. Here, children are free to be children. They live a completely carefree and happy existence, playing with toys, using their imagination, having their every whim catered to. Here, the lifestyle is determined by the child, not by outside, adult sources. If a child wants to wear the same costume for weeks on end? No problem. We'll launder it for them. If a child chooses to eat without silverware? That's fine with us."

I watched Dr. Carrini in amazement, thinking of Justin's behavior when he'd first turned up at the hospital—he'd seemed a little wild, a little unsure how to interact with people. And he hadn't used silverware. It was all making sense.

"So these kids are never unhappy?" I asked. I was thinking about Alice and how she'd wanted to escape with me, to find her brother.

Dr. Carrini's eyes narrowed. "They are never unhappy, except when they remember their old lives. And if stubborn unhappy memories pop up . . . well . . ."

I knew where this was going. "Well?"

Dr. Carrini's eyes met mine, cold and hard. "We offer them some pharmaceutical relief."

I nodded. "Drugs. You drug children."

His eyes flashed. "We use pharmaceuticals to help them deal with their problems. Just like a psychiatrist will prescribe drugs to a schizophrenic patient."

"But these kids aren't schizophrenics," I pointed out. "They're just kids who miss their parents."

Dr. Carrini glared at me. "I see that we have a different understanding of the issue," he said, his voice cool. "I have some people you should meet."

Dr. Carrini grabbed my arm, pulling me off the gurney and dragging me out of the operating room. I cast one glance back at Justin and Detective Cole, both of whom seemed to still be out cold. Dr. Carrini led me down the hall to a part of the bunker I'd never seen before. He pushed me through the doorway of a brightly lit room decorated in cheery colors. As my eyes adjusted to the light, I realized that a gaggle of kids and teenagers were here, playing and hanging out.

Dr. Carrini smiled. "Frank, allow me to introduce you to Kyle, Ellie, Luke, Tommy, Alice, and Kerry."

My blood ran cold. This was all of them—every member of the Misty Falls Lost—except for Justin and poor little Sarah. They looked up at me, some looking curious, some wary. Dr. Carrini was right about one thing, though—they looked happy. At least on the outside.

"Children," Dr. Carrini said, "please tell my friend Frank how happy you are to live here."

The children stared at me for a moment, and then Kerry, one of the older girls, spoke up. "Oh, we're very happy," she said. "We can do whatever we want here!"

"We play all day," a younger boy who I thought was Kyle added. "No school!"

"And nobody telling us what to do," a slightly older boy, Luke, explained.

My mind was spinning. Could these kids possibly be telling the truth? I sputtered, "B-but how happy can you be? Taken away from your families and forced to live in an underground bunker . . . never seeing daylight . . ."

The kids looked concerned, like they didn't understand what I was saying and were worried about me. Before I could explain, Dr. Carrini gestured to Scar and Baby Doc, who were watching the kids in the room, to pull me out. Within seconds I was being dragged down the hall, the doctor following. Hoping the kids would overhear, I shouted, "What do they think happened to Sarah? Do they know you killed her for asking too many questions, like you tried to kill Justin?"

Dr. Carrini's face clouded over. "She had an abnormal reaction to drugs," he said slowly and calmly, but I could tell I'd upset him. "It was an unavoidable tragedy."

"Meaning she was a problem for you, so you pumped drugs into her until she died?" I shouted again, hoping the kids were still listening. Dr. Carrini's face darkened.

"Did you kill Farley?" I shouted now. "Did he get too close to your little underground lair? Or how about Bailey? Did those two innocent people count as people you'd never *intentionally* hurt?"

The doctor's face was nearly purple now. I gulped; from his reaction, I was pretty sure my assertions were right.

"*Shut up,*" he hissed, sticking a finger in my face. "Their lives were sacrificed to keep the peace in Happyland. To save these children's childhoods!"

A chill ran up my spine. Dr. Carrini was even crazier than I'd thought he was, if he was willing to murder to keep his beloved "Happyland" safe.

Baby Doc and Scar dragged me back into the OR, where Justin and Detective Cole were still lying. I struggled to break free, but they shoved me back onto a gurney. Dr. Carrini drew closer, glaring at me and pulling a syringe from his lab coat pocket. "I think this is the end of your investigation," he said in a grave voice.

I felt ice down my spine. Was this it? Could it really end like this?

Dr. Carrini held up the syringe, pushing the plunger so a tiny drop of liquid appeared on the needle. I could see Scar and Baby Doc glancing at each other like they couldn't believe what they were seeing. Chloe, who had followed us down the hall and back, looked from me to the syringe and then quickly looked away.

Just then there was a horrible, deafening noise above—like someone shooting into metal!

"What the . . . ?" muttered Baby Doc, as everyone turned to look up.

"It's the entrance," Dr. Carrini said. "Someone's out there. Boys . . . hurry! Chloe, watch your friend till I return."

Putting the syringe back in his lab coat, Dr. Carrini hustled out with the two young doctors.

Going In

" I 'm against them!" I sputtered, feeling the sharp blade kiss my skin. "I'm with you! I'm trying to save my brother."

Smith smiled, removing the knife from my throat and loosening his grip.

I let out a huge sigh. "What," I demanded, "are you doing here? The last time I saw you, you were threatening Detective Cole's job."

Smith shook his head, still grinning. "Correction," he said. "*Jacob Greer* was threatening Detective Cole's job."

"Isn't that your client?" I asked, shaking my head. "I seem to recall you at that meeting, making just as big a stink as he was."

Smith nodded thoughtfully. "At the time, I agreed with him that you and your brother were troublemakers. You stole my bike, after all."

I gulped. "Yeah," I muttered, looking away. "Sorry about that."

Smith shrugged. "It's a small thing. Anyway, the truth is, that same night you stole my bike, I witnessed something unusual in the forest. While I was hidden in a patch of blackberry bushes, a couple of men ran by me in, of all things, hospital scrubs."

I gulped. Hospital scrubs? That sounded a lot like the orderlies Frank had described in the bunker.

"They seemed agitated," Smith went on. "Babbling to themselves about escape, and controlling the kids. When I heard your story the next day," he went on, taking in a breath, "I had to admit that what I'd witnessed made that seem plausible."

It took a minute for that to sink in. "Wait a minute," I said. "You believed us the whole time?"

Smith shrugged. "Secretly," he said, "I had to admit that what you described seemed . . . possible. At least enough for me to check out on my own. So this afternoon I made my move. I broke into Farley's cabin to look for clues."

"Um, isn't that illegal?" I asked. I was kind of

hoping the police would show up soon, because I was beginning to doubt the sanity of this guy. "And directly in violation of the wishes of your client?"

Smith snorted. "Son, I have a higher calling. The law and the wishes of my client must take a backseat to the truth."

I just stared at him. "Okay," I said finally. "Did you find anything at Farley's?"

"Nothing," he admitted, "so I moved on to Bailey's cabin, figuring that she had been murdered for a reason—most likely because she had information she wasn't supposed to. And there, I lucked out. I found her private laptop. In her e-mails to her supervisor, she'd made extensive notes about 'markings' . . . and finally about a 'locked metal door' she found in the woods and thought should be investigated. 'Could this be related to the deaths?' her e-mail had asked. But she was dead within hours of sending it, so she never found out. Fortunately, *I* was on the case, so I took her notes to find this entrance to what I believe may be the underground lab your brother visited."

"Wow," I murmured. All this time, Smith had been working parallel to me, investigating the same thing? "Why didn't you contact Detective Cole and me? We could have worked together."

Smith snorted again. "I work alone," he replied.

"And I do a fine job of it, I must say. Because here we are at the entrance to the bunker."

"Exactly," I said pointedly. "Here *we* are. I found this place too, via notes from Farley and Alice, one of the Lost kids. And the police are on their way."

"The police?" Smith frowned. "Well, we'd better get moving then." He pulled something out of his waistband that shone in the dim light. I looked down and started; it was a pistol.

"Are you *armed*?" I asked.

"And dangerous," Smith agreed cheerfully. "When you're in the service of the truth, you'd better have all the advantages available, don't you agree?" He leaned down suddenly, and I backed up, not trusting this guy at all. But then he straightened out, having pulled a smaller gun from a holster on his ankle. He held it out to me. "Fortunately for you, I always carry a spare."

I swallowed. "Um, thanks," I said, glancing from the cave to the woods and back to Smith. "I think we should wait for the police, though. You know, they're licensed to use their weapons."

Smith scowled. "I'm *licensed*," he insisted, like I'd made a playground taunt. "And between the two of us, we probably have more experience fighting crime than the rest of those bozos put together.

Oh yes," he went on, when he saw my jaw drop. "I know who you really are. Joseph Hardy, elite ATAC agent. Your brother, too. I didn't get my PI license from a gumball machine, you know." He grinned smugly.

I wasn't sure what else to say. "I really think we should wait for backup."

Smith sneered. "Those idiots will hurt us more than they'll help us. Look how they've botched the investigation so far."

Well, he had me there. With the exception of Detective Cole, I didn't exactly trust the Misty Falls PD. Not only had they failed to find any true leads about the Misty Falls Lost, they'd turned on Cole and me this morning. And I *was* a little concerned, I had to admit, about how they'd go about investigating a bunker they'd been convinced didn't exist.

"We don't know how many people are down there," I pointed out. "You go in shooting or whatever, you could incite an army. They could overpower the two of us and then what? Then the police are our only hope of saving everyone in the bunker."

Smith ignored me, looking up at the sky. "It's almost dark," he said, "and your brother is in imminent danger. Who knows what they're doing to him down there? Are you willing to risk his safety for a little backup?"

He held the gun out to me again. I didn't take it. I looked into the woods; still no sign of the police.

"I'm going in," said Smith, placing the smaller gun on the ground in front of me. "I'll leave you to make your own decisions. But this underground prison cell isn't operating for one second longer. Not on Smith's watch!"

With that, he spun around and, brandishing his pistol, charged toward the cave.

My heart jumped. "Smith!" I called. "Wait! Don't do it! You could make things worse!"

If he heard me at all, he gave no indication. He didn't even slow his pace. He was maybe ten yards from the cave now.

I looked back at the woods. No sign of the police, only dead silence. I swallowed hard and looked down at the gun Smith had left at my feet. This was *insane*. I had to be out of my mind to follow a narcissistic, arrogant, clearly unhinged PI—who'd spent part of the day working *against* me—into a mysterious bunker filled with unspeakable danger. And yet . . . the only other option was to let him go down there himself. With a big gun, an attitude, and serious delusions of grandeur. And my brother, my only brother, at the mercy of those inside.

I took a deep breath and picked up the gun. "Wait, Smith!" I called, running after him before I could think better of it. "I'm coming!"

Inside the cave, Smith had strapped on a head-lamp that he'd gotten from who-knows-where and was pulling rocks away from a little alcove in the rear of the cave. I looked into the alcove, and sure enough, a reinforced metal door lay within. I helped Smith move the rocks until we had a good view of the door. Smith pulled out his gun.

"What are you doing?" I asked, at the same time Smith fired a hail of bullets, shooting up the lock.

"Aaauuugh!" I cried, ducking down to avoid the bullets ricocheting off the metal. "They'll hear you! They're going to know we're coming now!"

But Smith had stopped firing and was staring at the door, smiling. He gestured to the lock. Sure enough, it hung open, obliterated by a ring of bullet holes.

Before I could speak, Smith disappeared through the door, and I heard him running down a hallway. I moved to follow him, but when I opened the door and peered down a dimly lit tunnel, he was already out of sight. I moved slowly and quietly down the tunnel, hoping that if the inhabitants had heard Smith's attack, they would find him and assume he was alone, buying me a little time.

At the end of the tunnel, I heard it.

"And just who are you?" a deep male voice demanded. I snuck a little farther down the tunnel, getting close enough to peer around the corner. Just a few feet ahead, the leather-jacket-wearing Smith, still with the headlamp, was facing off against two twentysomething men in hospital scrubs.

"I'm Michael Smith, PI," Smith replied, not sounding the least bit threatened, "and I've figured all this out! I know the truth of what goes on down here, and you're finished! Finished, do you hear me? Smith always gets his man! This little operation is done for, DONE FOR—"

BANG!!

I started as suddenly a shot was fired from behind the two doctors, taking Smith down. I stood silently watching as a new figure entered the scene, gun in hand—*Dr. Carrini!*

Dr. Carrini turned calmly to the two in scrubs, as if he hadn't just shot an intruder in cold blood. "Check the hatch, boys, and hide Mr. Smith until we can dispose of him. Chop-chop."

Without hesitating, the two men began walking swiftly toward the corner—where I was hiding. I looked around frantically, wondering if I would have to back out the way I'd come, but then

I spotted a small closet off the hall and darted in, managing to wedge myself into a corner.

"See anything?" one of the men asked the other.

"No, but we'd better keep looking. I'll check the hatch, you look in that closet. Okay?"

I felt my heart squeeze in my chest but forced myself to remain still. The door to the closet opened, and I saw the larger, baby-faced man peer in. He looked around at the mops, work suits, and cleaning supplies that filled the space. I pushed myself farther into the corner, praying that I was obscured by the hanging work suits.

The man slammed the door. "All clear here," he called to his partner.

Relief flooded through me as I breathed out.

But what now?

Science and Logic

I glanced over at Justin and Detective Cole, wondering if either was conscious. If there was any possibility for backup, I sure could use it now. But both were motionless, breathing heavily. I shivered. How long did I have before Dr. Carrini came back to finish me off?

"It didn't have to come to this, you know." I almost started at the cold voice, but turned around to see Chloe watching me intently. "I liked you," she continued. "You seemed like a smart person— a practical person. Someone who likes science and logic, like I do."

"I do," I said, looking at her and wondering how I ever could have thought I had feelings for her. "The difference between you and me is, I also have a heart."

Chloe winced. "That's not fair, Frank."

"Isn't it?" I asked, sitting up on the gurney. "How could you possibly be involved in this, Chloe? Taking kids away from their parents? You sat there in that hospital and watched Edie and Jacob cry over their son, and the whole time you knew what had really happened to him, knew he had been stolen away from them and raised by strangers. How could someone with a heart do that?"

She glared at me. "It's not like that, Frank. We care about the children here. We give them the childhood they deserve."

"And what happens when they're no longer children anymore?" I demanded. "When they get to be Justin's age, wanting to know where they came from and where their family went? What does Dr. Carrini do with them then?"

Chloe looked at me blankly, and the uncertainty in her face chilled me more than any answer could have.

"You don't *know?*" I asked incredulously.

"It's—it's a plan in transition," she sputtered, her mouth hardening into a frown. "We were looking at many different scenarios. We thought of educating the children to work with new recruits here. . . ."

"Keeping them prisoners here forever?" I shot back. "Never letting them see the sun?"

Chloe scowled. "It's not *like* that, Frank!" she cried. "You talk like being down here is so hard for them, so painful. But it's wonderful! It's—it's the childhood I never had!"

I looked at her curiously. Seeing my expression change, she paused.

"I was a foster kid," she admitted quietly after a moment. "Shuttled from family to family, no one to really pay attention to me. I *wish* someone like Dr. Carrini had found me and taken me away when I was little. I might have been able to play, to grow and enjoy life, instead of . . ." She trailed off, and then turned to face me again, her eyes burning with new intensity. "It's a good thing, what Dr. Carrini is doing. He really is a visionary!"

I sighed. "But Chloe," I said, trying to soften my tone, "don't you see? It's gone too far, this whole thing. Kids dying . . . parents like Edie losing their kids . . . is that part of the perfect childhood you would want for them?"

Chloe's expression changed, and she seemed to be considering my words.

BANG!!

We both started at the sound of a gunshot in the hall. A flash of fear passed over Chloe's face, and she turned back to me with renewed suspicion.

"Lie back down on your gurney," she barked. "I know you're just trying to find my weak spot so you can overpower me . . . but you can't overpower us! Do you see? You and whoever's trying to break in up there—we'll beat you!" She reached into her lab coat pockets, pulling out two items. "I have a taser and powerful drugs that would drop you in an instant!"

A *taser?* I hadn't seen that coming. And drugs . . . I wasn't sure she'd have the guts to give me anything that would permanently hurt me, but still, I held up my hands, giving in. "Okay. Okay. I know when I'm beat." I lay back down and stared at the ceiling for a moment, then chanced a quick look at Justin and started. I could swear I saw a finger move—a tiny motion, just enough to signal that he was aware of what was happening. Was it possible? Could Justin have been conscious and listening this whole time?

Whether or not he was, he might just be my only hope of getting out of here in one piece.

I took a deep breath. "If I were going to overpower you, Chloe," I said slowly, "I would do it . . . *now!*"

From that point on, everything happened very

quickly. Sure enough, Justin jumped up off his gurney, fully conscious, and together we leaped up to surround Chloe, easily forcing her to drop the taser and taking her syringes.

"The purple," Justin instructed me. "Give her the purple, it will make her sleep."

I looked down at the syringes I'd taken from Chloe: Sure enough, there was one full of the "purple" Alice and Justin had told me about. I held it up.

"No, Frank," Chloe begged. We had her backed into a corner now, and she looked suddenly very small and helpless. All of her earlier coldness and bravado were gone. "Please! You and I were connecting . . . I could be on your side. . . ."

I looked at her for a moment, her pretty face, her sad, lonely eyes. Then I injected her with the purple syringe. "I'm sorry, Chloe."

Within seconds, she fell to the ground, unconscious.

I looked at Justin. "What now?"

"We need to get the others!" he told me. "They'll help. At least a few of them will."

Shoving the taser and remaining syringes into Justin's pockets, we ran out of the OR and down the hallway to the playroom Dr. Carrini had taken me to earlier. Sure enough, all the same kids as before were gathered there, looking scared and unsure. They were completely unsupervised, which made me think that Baby Doc, Scar, and Dr. Carrini were all involved in whatever battle was going on upstairs.

"Listen," Justin announced, wasting no time. "Someone's broken in here, I don't know who. They're probably here to save him"—he pointed to me—"but they'll save us, too, if we help them. We just need to tell them the truth about this place, and we could all be free! Free to go back to our families and live normal lives."

Kerry, a pretty teen with red hair, started to cry. "Normal?" she asked. "I haven't felt normal in . . . so long."

"Then think how good it will feel," Justin said soothingly. "Our parents—they remember us. I can tell you for sure. I saw mine on the outside. They remember us, and they still love us. We have time to be families again."

I stepped forward. "Earlier, when you guys told me how happy you were here," I reminded them, "you were lying, weren't you? Because when I said that about missing your families . . ."

"Of course we were," said Luke, an older boy with sandy hair. "We can't tell the truth in front of the Big Boss, or he'll give us the purple."

"And we don't want the big sleep," added a familiar voice, and Alice stepped to the front of the group, still clad in her princess gown. "I'm glad you came back, Frank."

The kids looked at one another. "I want to be normal," one of the younger boys whispered.

"Me too," agreed Kerry, wiping away her tears. "We'll help you guys. We'll do everything we can."

With Justin's help, we got everybody armed with makeshift weapons: plastic baseball bats, a toy hammer, pots from the kitchen. Justin handed me the taser. The kids, Justin, and I moved out into the hall, where we were surprised to see Baby Doc and Scar approaching. They looked at our makeshift army in alarm, and Justin and I turned to each other.

"Attack!" I cried, and all the kids moved forward as one. The docs ran, but they were easily overpowered. For several minutes it was total chaos, kids beating on the doctors with plastic baseball bats and pans, while Justin struggled to inject Scar and Baby Doc with purple syringes and I stood by with the taser. It was hard to get to them in the melee, but finally he jabbed them both in the arm, and they went limp instantly.

Then, suddenly, a voice cut through all the chaos. "You are all in very big trouble with Daddy."

I looked up from the fracas. It was Dr. Carrini at the end of the hall, and he had a gun pointed at all of us. *They call him Daddy? Creepy . . .*

"Stop!" I cried, stepping in front of the kids. "You would never shoot, would you? You would never hurt the precious children you worked so hard to get."

Dr. Carrini stepped closer, and I shivered when I saw his eyes. They were cold, matter-of-fact . . . completely devoid of emotion. "It's a calculated risk, Frank," he explained, strolling closer. "If they persist in this attack and I have to fire, I may hurt one or two of the children, but Happyland will survive, and that's much more important."

Chills ran down my spine as I realized just how insane this guy was. He didn't even care about the kids themselves—just his crazy idea of preserving "childhood" (or his warped version of it) forever.

I looked at Justin, seeing the same realization in his eyes. We had to give up—we couldn't risk the kids' safety, even if it meant possibly defeating Dr. Carrini and ending Happyland forever.

I took a deep breath and turned back to the doctor—just as a figure appeared behind him.

It was *Joe.* He was sneaking up behind Dr. Carrini. And he had a gun. (Where'd he get that?)

"But . . . ," I began, just to get something out of my mouth, to keep the doctor talking so he wouldn't turn around and see my brother. "But what good would Happyland be with no children in it?"

Dr. Carrini chuckled. "Oh, Frank. You're so naive." He shrugged. "I can get children any time I want. Of course, it's easier during the summer camping season."

So creepy. "Like you got me?" I asked. "Hitting me over the head in the wee hours of the morning, dragging me back here?"

Dr. Carrini smirked. "You were one of the harder ones to acquire, Frank, what with your brother always around." He paused. "Of course, like I told you then, you're a little old for my collection."

Joe held up the gun, and I sucked in my breath.

BANG!

The bullet was only a warning shot, but it grazed Carrini's ear and startled him enough to drop his gun to the floor with a clatter. Justin and I rushed forward at the same time as Joe, and together the three of us tackled Carrini, Justin jabbing him violently with a purple syringe.

The kids cheered loudly. We'd done it!

Joe looked at me. "Frank, bro! I was beginning to think I'd never see you again. Are you okay?"

I nodded a little shakily. "Uh . . . yeah. It's been a weird few days."

Joe chuckled. "To say the least," he agreed.

I looked down at his hand. "Where'd you get the gun?"

"Long story."

Suddenly, over all the cheering and craziness, a voice called down the hatch. "Hello? Joe? Are you there?"

Joe grinned at me. "That'll be the Misty Falls PD," he explained. "Down here!" he shouted back toward the entrance.

Within minutes, the crazy scene had gotten even crazier. Six uniformed police officers rushed in, looking around like they couldn't believe what they were seeing.

"Holy . . . ," one of the officers muttered when he turned the corner and saw Joe and me standing over an unconscious Dr. Carrini, the group of kids behind us. "What *is* this place?"

"It's kind of a long story," I replied. "How long do you have?"

In broad strokes, I filled them—and my brother—in on everything I'd learned about the underground bunker: who built it, what Dr. Carrini was doing with it, how the kids were treated. I could tell the officers were having trouble believing it was all true, but the kids backed up my story. The officers cuffed Dr. Carrini, Baby Doc, Scar, and Chloe, in case the "purple" wore off and they woke up. They also rounded up several other guards who'd been working for Dr. Carrini in the bunker. When the coast was clear, they called up the hatch: "All right! You two can come on down!"

We waited as footsteps approached, and then around the corner stepped . . . Justin's parents.

They both started sobbing with relief at the sight of Justin. "I'm sorry," whispered Jacob, throwing his arms around his son. "I'm so sorry I didn't believe you boys."

As the Greers reunited with lots of tears and hugging, the officers explained that while they had initially doubted my story—and Joe's, since he believed me—they had rethought their earlier position, took Joe's call about the hatch location seriously, and told Edie and Jacob they were fairly sure where Justin was being held.

The officer who explained this all to me looked sheepish. "I guess some things that seem too crazy to be true . . . aren't."

I looked around the underground tunnels, the OR, the crazy playroom, and the kids. "Sometimes," I told him, "I think the craziest things are the truest."

Imperfect

"I'm going to need you to pass me another square of chocolate, bro," I said, carefully inserting my toasted marshmallow between two graham crackers for the ultimate in s'more goodness.

Frank tossed me the bag. "I'd ask how you can eat like that after all we've been through," he said with a smirk, "but then I remember who I'm talking to."

I grinned. Between us, our campfire crackled comfortingly. We were back in Misty Falls State Park, camping for one more night before we caught a plane back to Bayport. It was a perfect night, clear and cool. And now that we had gotten to the bottom of our case, we felt we could really enjoy the park's beauty without being insanely freaked out by every bump in the night.

Maybe I should speak for myself there.

"It feels good, doesn't it?" asked Frank with a smile. "Knowing all those kids are back with their families tonight. So many happy reunions."

I nodded. "It feels great," I agreed. "Although I still think about poor little Sarah. Or Farley and Bailey. So many people died unnecessarily, just to feed Carrini's crazy vision of what childhood should be."

Frank nodded, wrinkling his nose. "All play and no reality. No parents. No rules. I'd prefer our childhood, wouldn't you?" he asked.

"Big-time," I agreed, popping my s'more in my mouth.

Frank grinned again. "Well, at least Smith survived."

I snorted. Michael Smith was currently resting at Misty Falls Hospital, recovering from an operation to remove the bullet that had missed his heart and lodged in his shoulder. According to Detective Cole, Smith was in good spirits and trying to take credit for solving the whole case. He'd also asked for some of Cole's officers to go looking for his bike, which, sadly, was thus far still missing somewhere in the wilds of the state park.

Detective Cole was alive and well, after having a monster nap due to a big dose of "purple." While we'd been searching Farley's cabin earlier, Baby Doc and Scar had snuck in, jabbed Detective Cole with a syringe, and dragged him out. They'd managed to jab him before he even realized he was being watched, which is why he hadn't made a sound.

It turned out that Baby Doc and Scar were both relatives of Dr. Carrini's, and victims of the "imperfect" childhoods Carrini was so obsessed with. He'd taken them in, given them minor medical training, and put them to work at Happyland to give them some measure of the childhood he'd thought they deserved. Unfortunately, they were not supercompetent—which explained why they'd only picked up Detective Cole, and not me. Lucky for all of us they were lousy kidnappers, otherwise Michael Smith, who'd turned out to be reckless as well as conceited, might have been our only hope.

"I hope Detective Cole gets some rest tonight," I said. "After all he went through today."

Frank nodded. "Although I'm glad he's getting his due from the town."

This evening the mayor of Misty Falls had announced that Detective Cole would be getting a medal from the town in a special ceremony tomorrow, to thank him for all his hard work on the Misty Falls Lost case, and for never giving up. The detective had seemed pleased, but more than anything, I think he was glad the kids had been found and this case was finally behind him. "I can sleep tonight," he'd told us when he dropped us off at the campsite, "and not feel guilty. I really can't thank you boys enough for all your help."

Justin Greer, and all the Misty Falls Lost, had been taken to the hospital for observation, but they all seemed to be in good health. It would be a long adjustment back to "normal" life—with a lot of counseling for the kids and their families—but they were on their way. All the parents had been called, and Justin was eager to spend time with his real parents again. He said he was recovering some new memories of them, and they all seemed so happy to be reunited. Justin would live with Edie and Hank but would spend summers and holidays with Jacob and Donna.

"I'm glad Jacob apologized to Detective Cole," Frank added. "He certainly deserved it."

"Yeah," I agreed. "I have to admit, this case was full of surprises, but for me one of the biggest ones was that Jacob wasn't involved in Happyland."

Frank nodded. "I was a little surprised too. He

was unpredictable. But I guess he was just a dad struggling with his emotions and his responsibility to his son. This can't have been easy for him."

"No," I agreed, "and I don't think it will be easy for any of the parents. Dr. Carrini took a lot away from them."

Frank looked like he was going to respond, but just then we heard a crash over to our left.

I looked at my brother with wide eyes. "Frank," I snapped. "Don't try to be funny."

"Funny?" asked my bro, looking nervously over to the left. "Who's trying to be funny? I didn't make that noise."

"There's nothing out here," I said, trying to convince myself more than him. "We solved the case. It's all over."

Frank opened his mouth to respond, but then there was another crash—closer this time. He stood quickly, and I followed suit.

"Come on," he whispered, and together we backed into the woods and fell silent.

The noises came closer, and I felt like my heart would pound out of my chest. But then something emerged from the trees at the far side of our campground—a female black bear! I looked at Frank, whose eyes were just as huge as mine, but he gestured to me to be silent. I turned back to the campsite, where the female was now joined by two young cubs. They sniffed around our campsite, overturning bags and pawing at our tent, ripping open the bag of chocolate and devouring what was left of that, the graham crackers, and the marshmallows. After a few more minutes of searching, the mother called to the two cubs, and they sauntered back into the woods the way they'd come. Frank and I stood silent and reverent, waiting a few minutes before turning to each other.

"I guess Farley was right about one thing," Frank said quietly. "Nature really *is* beautiful—but it deserves respect."

"Absolutely," I said, shaking my head in amazement. "And as we've learned, the wilderness can be dangerous—in more ways than one."

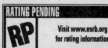